# HITTY
## Her First Hundred Years

# HITTY
## Her First Hundred Years

# RACHEL FIELD

#### with illustrations by
## Dorothy P. Lathrop

**ALADDIN PAPERBACKS**

First Aladdin Paperbacks edition September 1998

Aladdin Paperbacks
An imprint of Simon & Schuster Children's Publishing Division
1230 Avenue of the Americas
New York, NY 10020

Library of Congress Catalog Card Number 98-73305

ISBN-13: 978-0-689-82284-1
ISBN-10: 0-689-82284-7
1013 OFF

This Book Is Dedicated to
**The State of Maine**
and
**Abbie Evans**

# Contents

# Illustrations

# HITTY
## Her First Hundred Years

## ❧ CHAPTER I ❧
# In Which I Begin My Memoirs

The antique shop is very still now. Theobold and I have it all to ourselves, for the cuckoo clock was sold day before yesterday and Theobold has been so industrious of late there are no more mice to venture out from behind the woodwork. Theobold is the shop cat—the only thing in it that is not for sale, which has made him rather overbearing at times. Not that I wish to be critical of him. We all have our little infirmities and if it had not been for his I might not now be writing my memoirs. Still, infirmities are one thing, and claws are another, as I have reason to know.

Theobold is not exactly a bad cat, but he is far from considerate. Besides, he is prowlishly inclined and he has the most powerful claws and tail I have ever known. Then, just lately he has taken to sleeping in the shop window with his head on the tray of antique jewelry. If Miss Hunter could have seen how narrowly he missed swallowing one of the garnet earrings when he yawned night before last, she would be very uneasy indeed. But Miss Hunter has had Theobold ever since she opened the antique shop and she seems to set great store by him for his trying ways. Miss Hunter has a good many queer ones of her own and I must say that I felt a little *wadgetty,* as Phoebe Preble's mother used to say, at first over her habit of poking and peering and turning everything upside down. One grows used to this in time, though it wasn't what I was brought up to consider the best manners. But Miss Hunter means well and if she decides you are genuine there is nothing she will not do for you. That is why after she found me knocked off my chair and on my nose three different mornings she said she would run no chances with such a valuable old doll but would take me out of the window each night before shutting up shop.

So here I am in the midst of her very untidy desk with my feet on a spattered square of green blotting paper, my back against a pewter inkstand, and a perfect snow bank of bills and papers heaped about me. Nearby, weighting down another pile of scribbled sheets, is an old conch shell. I have seen far handsomer ones in my time; still, it is a reminder. I cannot see the light shine on its curving sides without thinking of the Island in the South Seas and all the adventures that befell us there. Across the store on the mantelpiece is the model of a sailing vessel, square-rigged, in a glass bottle. But its sails are not so well trimmed, and its gilding not so fine as the *Diana-Kate's* when we sailed out of Boston Harbor. Perhaps tonight the old Swiss music box will begin to play all of itself, as it does sometimes without the least warning. It is strange to sit here and listen while it tinkles out the "Roses and Mignonette" waltz with the same precise gaiety as in the days when Isabella Van Rensselaer and the rest danced to that tune at Monsieur Pettoe's select salon for young ladies and gentlemen. That was just across Washington Square, scarcely a block away from where I sit today, but there were no skyscrapers then nor any street of little shops like this.

It may have been the ship in the bottle, or it may have been
the music box, though I think it more likely that the quill pen
gave me the idea of writing the story of my life. The pen
belongs with the pewter inkstand, but quills are as much out
of fashion today as whalebones in ladies' dresses and poke
bonnets for little girls. Still, one cannot forget one's early training, and not for nothing did I watch Clarissa copy all those
mottoes into her exercise book with a quill pen. If it is true, as
Miss Hunter and the Old Gentleman declare, that I am the
most genuine antique in the shop, why should I not prefer
quills to these new-fangled fountain pens? Nor am I inclined
to scratchy steel affairs with sharp points. So I will be true to
my quill pen which I now take in hand to begin my memoirs.

I begin my memoirs.

As far as I can learn, I must have been made something over a hundred years ago in the State of Maine in the dead of winter. Naturally I remember nothing of this, but I have heard the story told so often by one or another of the Preble family that at times it seems I, also, must have looked on as the Old Peddler carved me out of his piece of mountain-ash wood. It was a small piece, which accounts for my being slightly undersized even for a doll, and he treasured it greatly, for he had brought it across the sea from Ireland. A piece of mountain-ash wood is a good thing to keep close at hand, for it brings luck besides having power against witchcraft and evil. That was the reason he had carried this about in the bottom of his pack ever since he had started peddling. Mostly he did his best business from May to November when roads were open and the weather not too cold for farmers' wives and daughters to stand on their doorsteps as he spread out his wares. But that year he tramped farther north than he had ever been before. Snow caught him on a road between the sea and a rough, woody country. The wind blew such a gale it heaped great drifts across the road in no time and he was forced to come knocking at the kitchen door of the Preble House, where he had seen a light.

Mrs. Preble always said she didn't know how she and Phoebe would have got along without the Old Peddler, for it took all three of them, besides Andy the chore-boy, to keep the fires going and to water and feed the horse, the cow, and the chickens in the barn. Even when the weather cleared, the roads were impassable for many days and all vessels storm-bound in Portland Harbor. So the Peddler decided to stay on and help with odd jobs round the place till spring, since Captain Preble was off on his ship for months to come.

At that time, Phoebe Preble was a little girl of seven with gay and friendly ways and fair hair that hung in smooth, round curls on either side of her face. It was for her that I was transformed from a piece of mountain-ash wood only six and a half inches high, not nearly so tall as a bayberry candle, into a doll of parts. My first memories, therefore, are of a square pleasant room with brown beams and a great fireplace like a square cave, where flames licked enormous logs of wood and an old black kettle hung from an iron crane. The first words I ever heard were Phoebe's as she called to her mother and Andy: "See, now the doll has a face!" They came over to peer at me as the Old Peddler held me between his thumb and forefinger, turning me this way and that in the firelight so my paint would dry. I can remember Phoebe's excitement over my features and her mother's amazement that the old man had been able to give such a small bit of wood a real nose and even a pleasant expression. Surely no one, they all agreed, had so much skill with a jackknife. That night I was left to dry on the mantelpiece with the light from the dwindling fire making strange shadows, with mice squeaking and scampering in and out of the walls, and the wind outside blowing through the branches of a great pine tree with the sound that I was to know so well later on.

Phoebe's mother had decided that I was not to be played with until properly clothed. Phoebe was not a child who took readily to sewing, but her mother was firm, so presently out came needles and thread, thimbles and piece-bag, and I was being measured for my first outfit. It was to be of buff calico strewn with small red flowers, and I thought it was very fine indeed. Phoebe's stitches were not always of the finest. She was apt to grow fidgetty after ten or fifteen minutes of sewing; still, she was so anxious to play with me that she quite surprised us all by her diligence. I do not remember exactly how I came by my name. At first, I was christened Mehitabel, but Phoebe was far too impatient to use so many syllables, and presently I had become Hitty to the whole household. Indeed, it was at Mrs. Preble's suggestion that these five letters were worked carefully in little red cross-stitch characters upon my chemise.

"There," said Phoebe's mother when the last one was done, "now whatever happens to her she can always be sure of her name."

"But nothing is ever going to happen to her, Mother!" cried the little girl, "because she will always be my doll."

How strange it seems to remember those words now! How little we thought then of all that was so soon to befall us!

Well, after some weeks I was finished and the last stitch set in my sprigged calico. Unfortunately, this took place on a Saturday and in those days most children were not allowed to play with their toys from sundown until the following evening. It was still February and the sun sank behind the spruce-covered hills across the road far too early to please Phoebe Preble. In vain she begged to play with me just another half hour by the fire. Her mother shut me away in the top drawer of an old pine dresser lest the sight of me should tempt my little mistress too much. Here I remained in seclusion beside Mrs. Preble's best Paisley shawl and Phoebe's own little sealskin muff and tippet that her father had brought home for her from his last trip to Boston until next morning when the preparations for churchgoing began.

These Sunday expeditions to church were of great importance to the Preble family, as they lived several miles away and it meant a long sleigh ride. Phoebe was dressed and ready long before her mother and Andy. By standing on a footstool she was able to open the dresser drawer and soon she was bending over me. She had come there to get out the furs, but the sight of me was too much for her, though in justice to Phoebe I must say that she tried to put temptation from her.

"No, Hitty," she said, "this is Sunday and so I must not touch you, not till after sunset tonight."

She sighed as she thought what a long way off that would be and before either of us realized what was happening she had me in her hands.

"After all," she told me apologetically, "Mother just said I mustn't play with you on Sunday and I am only smoothing your dress out."

But presently it occurred to her that I was just of a size to fit into her muff. In I must go, and once there it was not surprising that the plan should occur to her as it did.

"No one would guess that you were in my muff, Hitty," she whispered, and I could tell from the sound of her voice that I was not going to spend the rest of the morning in the pine dresser. Just then her mother came bustling in saying that they must start at once or they would be too late for the doxology. I had no idea then what a doxology might be, but the thought of missing it worried her so much that she took out her shawl without noticing my absence from the drawer or how very red Phoebe's cheeks had grown.

It was warm and cozy in the sealskin muff, though when Phoebe put both hands in it meant rather cramped quarters for me. I could see nothing, of course, except an occasional flicker of blinding brightness, which I knew must be sun on snow. Still, I could feel the motion of the horse pulling us over the road. I could hear the snow squeak and crackle under our runners, the whistle of the whip as the Old Peddler cracked it, and the gay tinkle-tankle of our sleigh bells. This sound was not to Mrs. Preble's liking, for she kept scolding Andy because he had forgotten to take them off the harness. She said it was not keeping the Sabbath day holy to go to church with bells on and she didn't know what the neighbors would think. But Andy said a bell was a bell and he couldn't see what difference it made whether it was on a sleigh or in a church steeple.

This remark caused Phoebe's mother to reprove him severely. She would have said more had the sleigh not drawn up to the steps just then. The idea that I was in church, in a place where dolls are not supposed to be under any circumstances, filled me with excited curiosity. Although still unable to see out of the muff, I managed to hear a good deal that went on. Even now, after all these years, I can still hear the rustle of the people rising about me and their voices singing all together:

*Praise God from whom all blessings flow,*
*Praise Him all creatures here below. . . .*

It made me feel solemn right down to the soles of my wooden feet.

The sermon and prayers were so long I gave up trying to follow them. As for Phoebe, she first grew fidgetty, then slumped back against her mother to take a nap. It was in this way that my mishap occurred. I suppose the muff was dangling from her hand as she slept. Gradually, her hold must have loosened, for next thing I knew I was falling headfirst out of my snug sealskin hiding-place to the floor. Fortunately, it happened just as the congregation rose for a last blessing, so no one heard me fall. The muff rolled in the opposite direction, to be rescued by Andy, and Phoebe was jerked to her feet to bow her head with the rest.

Frightened as I was, it never occurred to me that I should not be picked up again—not till I saw all the feet walking out of the Preble pew. I heard the sound of sleighs and horses at the doors, and still I hoped Phoebe would manage to return for me. But at last I heard doors being locked and shutters banged to, so I abandoned all hope of being saved. I knew Phoebe's mother must have hurried her out and now she did not dare confess that she had taken me to church. So I gave myself up to considering the sad state in which I found myself on my very first entry into the outside world.

Then there were the bats.

I do not greatly enjoy remembering the days and nights that followed, and to this day I have no idea how many there actually were. I only know that I have never been more miserable, not even when facing fire and shipwreck. The cold was fearful. It seemed as if my legs and arms would crack with it. The wind howled outside, nails snapped and beams creaked, and the old bell rope dangling in the vestibule swung to and fro with a dismal sound. Then there were the bats. I had been unprepared for them and there was one that made its home in the corner under the Preble pew only a few inches from where I lay. By day he hung himself in a gray ball, but at night he flew out and went swooping about in a way that terrified me. Sometimes his wings even touched me as he flew low, and I could see the shine of his little black eyes in the dark. His claws looked very sharp to me. I hoped I should have no occasion to feel them. Also, the discomfort of my lot was not helped any by an illustrated Bible which lay on the floor beside me, open at the most painful picture of a man being swallowed by a large fish. At the time, I felt that our two positions were equally unfortunate.

One day I grew hopeful at the sound of a key turning in the lock. It was the sexton making his midweek rounds to see that all was as it should be. Once more I began to be hopeful—but how to catch his attention? There I lay hidden under a pew, hemmed in by a footstool and a Bible, and unable to lift a finger to help myself. I say I was unable to lift a finger. I must confess that the Old Peddler had seen fit to give me only one on either hand, and that a thumb, with all the rest left in one solid piece like a mitten. I must therefore rely on my feet. These were pegged to my legs and I had also been denied the

There was a painful picture of a man
being swallowed by a large fish.

luxury of knees. Still, by exerting all my powers, I could make a clumsy motion from the upper pegs that fastened them to my body. I decided it was the only thing to do, so I raised and lowered them several times as best I could.

*Clump! Clump! Clump!*

Even I was startled by the noise they made thumping on the boards of the old floor. The sound echoed through the church in a positively terrifying manner. I heard the sexton give a smothered exclamation and drop what must have been his broom with a great clatter. Then he ran off toward the back of the church, bumping into pews as he went. I could hear him muttering in a scared sort of way:

"Maybe a ghost and maybe not, but I'm takin' no chances!"

Even in my own discomfort I could not but feel a thrill of pride that my two wooden feet could produce such an effect upon him.

Fortunately for me, Phoebe Preble was not good at keeping secrets to herself. Before the week was out she had confessed her disobedience in taking me to church and had promised to mend her ways if only I could be restored to her. Accordingly, she was set down to sew an extra long stint on her sampler, while Andy and the Old Peddler drove off to fetch me back.

No pen, not even the finest quill, could describe my joy at being once more in the midst of my family. No fire has ever seemed so bright and leaping as that in the Preble fireplace. How good to feel its warmth upon me and to see it making flickers of brightness on the shining pots and pans and on Phoebe's fair head, bent over the square of canvas upon which she was working this motto in cross-stitch:

*Conscience distasteful truths may tell,*

*But mark her sacred lesson well.*
*Whoever lives with her at strife*
*Loses his better friend for life.*

No wonder Phoebe and I knew it by heart, for her mother had decreed that I was not to be played with till the final *e* had been sewed in satisfactorily. This took many days, and there were tears and knottings of thread and much taking out and putting in of stitches.

I looked on sympathetically from an upper shelf to which I had been banished. This was to be a lesson to the little girl, and after hearing all the things Mrs. Preble told Phoebe about consciences and how careful one must be to listen and do as they said, I began to feel glad that dolls do not have them. I think Phoebe wished that she could lose hers, judging from the sighs I heard her give over the sampler.

꙳ ꙳ ꙳ ꙳

Spring was very late in coming to Maine that year. It was mid-March before the first thaw set in and for a month after that the road was a river of mud, so it was well-nigh impossible for horses and wagons to pass. The pussy willows were weeks behind their usual time. Andy could not make willow whistles till May. Then, suddenly, one day there were buds on the lilac bushes by the Preble door and in the woods across the road yellow and blue violets, snowdrops, and hepaticas. There were Mayflowers, too, if one knew where to find them, and Andy and Phoebe did. Often since then I have seen them in florists' windows, done up in stiff little bunches, so different from the trailing sprays of pink and white bloom we gathered in the Preble woods under last year's leaves and fir cones.

We gathered arbutus that spring in the Preble woods.

Once the roads were passable again, the Old Peddler set off with his pack and a big bag of food Mrs. Preble had cooked for him. Phoebe took me in her arms as she and Andy walked with him to the three-cornered island of grass where three roads met. There they said good-bye and watched him disappear down the one that led to Portland. He walked with a limp and his pack was so heavy it made him bend to one side, the way trees do if they grow in windy places. When he had reached the turn in the road, he stopped and waved to us. Andy and Phoebe waved back. They kept on doing it long after he was out of sight.

We should have felt very lonely without him if Phoebe's father had not turned up shortly after. He strode up the path between the lilac bushes without any warning, having driven over in a gig from Portland with so many boxes, bales, and sea chests that the front hall overflowed with them. Such treasures as they held, too—silks and Paisley shawls, carved ivories and corals, stuffed birds and knickknacks from every port he had touched at. I often wonder what Miss Hunter would say if she could see them.

Captain Preble was a big man, six feet four in his socks, as his wife always explained with pride, and he had the brightest blue eyes I have ever seen. When he laughed, they almost shut up tight and lots of little lines spread out at the corners like rays from the sun in old pictures. He laughed a great deal, too, especially at things Phoebe said. Whenever he did so it seemed as if the sound began at the toes of his enormous sea boots and went rumbling up and up till it came bursting out of his mouth in great ho-ho's.

Almost the first words that Phoebe said to her father, when

he had kissed her and swung her up over his head two or three times to see how big she had grown, were:—"This is my new doll, Hitty." Then he must hear all about the Old Peddler and the ash wood and how I had spent part of a week under their pew in church. At that Captain Preble laughed so hard the buttons on his coat heaved up and down like little ships at sea, in spite of the way Phoebe's mother shook her head at him.

"It isn't a laughing matter, Dan'l," she told him, "I declare I don't know where the good is of my trying to raise that child properly if you have her as spoiled as a popinjay inside a week."

I remember her very words, because I have never been able to discover what sort of bird a popinjay might be. One does not hear them mentioned nowadays, so I suppose the race must have died out years ago.

## CHAPTER II
# In Which I Go Up in the World
# and Am Glad to Come Down Again

I could fill many pages with accounts of that first summer—
of the trips we took with Captain Preble in his gig, to
Portland, Bath, and nearer farms; of the expeditions in the old
pumpkin-colored dory with the home-made canvas he was
teaching Andy to sail; and of the visits from neighbors and
relations who often came to spend all day now that the weather was so fine. Such long, blue, sunny days they were, too, and,
as happens in northern places where seasons are short, all the
flowers seemed to be trying to blossom at once. When butter-
cups and daisies and devil's paint brushes were still bright in
all the fields, the wild roses were already opening their petals,
and before their last one fell, Queen Anne's lace and early
goldenrod were beginning to crowd them out. Then there
were the baskets of berries to be picked. Never had there been
such a season for them, everyone said, especially for wild raspberries. Indeed, it was thanks to them that I was so nearly lost
to the world.

It came about in this way: Mrs. Preble had sent us off to
pick another quart or two for her preserving. Andy and Phoebe
were to go to a patch not more than a mile or so down the
road, where we had picked several days before. Andy carried a

All the flowers seemed to be trying to blossom at once.

big splint-bottomed basket, while Phoebe had a small one in which I was allowed to ride until it should be time for me to yield my place to the raspberries. She had lined it neatly with plantain leaves that felt pleasantly cool and smooth. It was a hot afternoon in late July, and I was thankful to be out of the dust and glare of the road. It seemed to me that this was one of the many times when it was nice to be a doll. Alas! How soon I was to change my opinion!

But when we reached the berry patch, someone had been before us. The bushes were bent and broken and there was hardly a raspberry left.

"There's a place 'way down by the shore," Andy remembered, just as they were turning away disappointed. "You go over to the Back Cove and walk along the beach till you come to a kind of clearing between the trees. Those raspberries are 'most as big as my two thumbs put together."

"But Mother said we weren't to go off the turnpike," Phoebe reminded him, "not out of sight of it, anyhow."

"Well," Andy wasn't one to give up anything he had his mind set on, "she sent us to get raspberries, didn't she? And there ain't any more here."

There was no denying this, and it took little urging to make Phoebe forget her mother's words. Soon we were headed for the Back Cove through a stretch of very thick spruce woods, with only a thread of a footpath between the close-packed trees.

"I heard Abner Hawks telling your ma last night that there's Injuns round again," Andy told Phoebe. "He said they was Passamaquoddies, a whole lot of 'em. They've got baskets and things to sell, but he said you couldn't trust 'em round the corner. We'd better watch out in case we see any."

Phoebe shivered.

"I'm scared of Injuns," she said.

"Come on," Andy urged, "here's where we turn off to the Cove. We have to walk a ways on the stones."

It was pretty rough going and the stones were well heated after hours in the hot sun. Phoebe complained of them even through her slippers, while Andy, who was barefooted, yelled and jumped from one to another. He kept running down to the water's edge and splashed about to cool his feet off, so that it was some time before they reached the raspberry patch and settled down to picking. Phoebe set me comfortably between the roots of a knotty old spruce tree at the edge of the clearing, where I could see them as they moved among the bushes. Sometimes the brambles grew so high that only their heads showed, like two round apples, one yellow and the other red, bobbing above the greenery.

It was very peaceful and pleasant there by the Back Cove. The spruce woods sloped down to the water, their tips as dark and pointed as hundreds of arrowheads against the sky. The Cove itself was blue and shining, with little white scallops of foam breaking round the edges of distant Cow Island. The air was filled with the sound of bees and birds, of the sea shuffling pebbles alongshore, and the voices of Andy and Phoebe calling to each other as they picked. No other doll in the world felt quite so contented as I.

Then suddenly, without the least warning, I heard Phoebe give a sharp cry.

"Injuns, Andy, Injuns!"

I saw her point toward the woods behind me. Her eyes and Andy's looked as round as doorknobs. But I saw nothing, for I could not turn my head around. Andy seized Phoebe's hand and began running with her in the opposite direction. Pebbles rattled under their feet as they sped along the shingle beach, and raspberries tumbled out of their baskets at every step. Then they disappeared among the trees without a single backward look. At first, I could not believe that they had forgotten me. But there was no doubt about it. It was awful to wait there alone, to hear twigs snapping and voices muttering behind me strange words I could not understand. But feeling things behind one is always so much more terrifying than when they actually appear.

They were only some five or six squaws in moccasins, beads, and blankets, who had come after raspberries, too. No one noticed me between the spruce roots. I watched them filling their woven baskets and thought they looked very fat and kind, though rather brown and somewhat untidy as to hair.

One of them had a papoose slung on her back, and its little bright eyes looked out from under her blanket like a woodchuck peering out of its hole. It was almost sunset when they paddled off through the trees again with their full baskets.

**Suddenly I felt myself hoisted into the air by my waistband.**

"Now," thought I to myself, "Andy and Phoebe will come back for me."

But I began to grow a little worried as the sun dropped lower and lower behind the trees. The sky was full of bright clouds now. Companies of sea gulls were flying off toward Cow Island. I could see the sunset on their wings as they moved. It would have seemed very beautiful to me if I had been in the proper company. I felt suddenly bereft and very small indeed. But this was nothing to what I was about to feel.

It happened so quickly that I have no very clear idea of how it actually came about. I had heard distant cawings all that afternoon and I had been vaguely aware that crows were in the nearby trees. But I was used to crows. There were plenty of them round the Preble house, so I thought little of their raucous "caw-caw's" till one sounded alarmingly near my head. At the same time I felt a curious blackness settling down upon me. I knew this could not be night for the sky was still pink, and besides, this blackness was heavy and warm. Nor was this all. Before I could do anything to save myself, a sharp, pointed beak was pecking at my face and the wickedest pair of yellow eyes I have ever seen were bent upon me. "Caw, caw, caw!"

Stout ash wood though I was, I quailed at the fierceness of this attack. I felt that my end had come and I was glad to bury my face in the cool moss so that I might be spared the sight of the Crow's cruel expression. Looking back upon it now, I realize that perhaps the Crow was not really cruel. Crows cannot help their blackness or their sharp beaks. But they should be all the more careful about what they seize. Evidently, this one was rather discouraged about eating me, for after several attempts it gave up trying. I could hear it giving vent to a rather unflattering opinion of its latest find in more loud "caw-caw's." But it was a very persistent Crow, determined to put me to some use.

Suddenly I felt myself hoisted into the air by my waistband. I tried to cling to the moss and tree roots, but it was no use. They sank away from me as I rose feet first. The Back Cove, the spruce woods, and the raspberry patch were a queer jumble under me. My skirts crackled in the wind as it rushed past, and now I felt myself go up, now down, according to the Crow's fancy.

"This is certainly the end of me!" I thought, expecting each moment to go spinning through space.

But strange, indeed, are the ways of Providence and of crows!

I came to rest at last and when I had collected my wits enough to look about I found myself in a great untidy nest at the top of a pine tree, staring into the surprised faces of three half-grown crows. If it had been trying to have one crow pecking and peering, it was still more so to have three all fighting over me at once. They may not have been so large and fierce as their mother, but they made up for this by their hoarse cries for food and their gaping red gullets. Their beaks were continually open and I even began to have more sympathy for the Mother Crow when I saw the amount of food she had to keep dropping down those yawning caverns. But hardly was a morsel swallowed before it was "squawk, squawk, squawk" again and off she must fly for more. Never have I seen such appetites, and I had plenty of time to see, for I must have spent the better part of two days and nights in that nest.

A more uncomfortable position I have never found myself in. The nest was large of its kind but not nearly big enough for three restless crows already nearing the fledgling stage. I was jostled and crowded and poked and shoved till it seemed there would be nothing left of me. To add to the crowded quarters the Mother Crow folded herself over the lot of us and I nearly suffocated down at the bottom of the nest with baby crows' claws scratching and sharp spikes of twig sticking into me.

How I ever survived that first night I do not know.

But morning came at last and the Mother Crow began her foragings for food. It was strange to see the sun rise behind the topmost branches of a pine, instead of through decent windowpanes, and to feel the nest rocking as the branches swayed in the wind. Rather a pleasant sensation when one grows used to it. This motion combined with the crows' jostlings made my position even more precarious, and I knew I must keep my feet braced firmly between the crisscross twigs if I did not wish to be crowded out. Little by little I learned to change my place and to climb higher so that I might peer out over the nest's edge. This terrified me at first, so that I dared not look down from such a vast height. That was why it took me such a long time to discover that I was not far from home, as I had supposed, but within a stone's throw of my own front door. The Crow had carried me to the very ancestral pine that grew beside the Preble house. I could scarcely believe my eyes when I saw the smoke rising from that familiar chimney and saw old knobble-kneed Charlie grazing near the barn.

There was comfort in this at first. Later, it seemed only to make things harder. To see the Preble family moving about below me, to hear the voices of Andy and Phoebe, and yet to be unable to attract their attention was tantalizing. And still the baby crows squawked and shoved and fought over the insides of mussel shells and sea urchins. I grew more uncomfortable and lonely as the day wore on.

Now I saw the sunset between pine needles. The wind moved through them with a deep, rushing noise. This may sound very beautiful when one listens to it in safety on firm ground, but it is a very different matter to hear it from such a perilous perch as mine. I could see curls of blue smoke going up from the Preble chimney and I knew supper must be cooking in the big fireplace. Soon they would be gathering round the table to eat it. But I should not be with them.

"Phoebe would certainly cry if she could see where her doll is now," I thought to myself disconsolately, poking my arm between two twigs as the most active of the crows jostled me.

I was none too quick, either, for the young crows were becoming more and more restless. They begrudged me even the smallest corner until I began to realize that my hours in their nest were numbered.

Night came on. The stars shone very clear and big, like snow crystals sprinkled across the dark. A despair settled down upon me, heavier than the Crow's wing, blacker than the night sky.

"I cannot bear it any longer," I told myself at last. "Better be splintered into kindling wood than endure this for another night."

I knew that any move must be made at once before the Mother Crow returned from a last late foraging expedition, so I began working my way toward the edge of the nest. I must confess that I have never been more frightened in my life than when I peered down into that vast space below and thought of deliberately hurling myself into it. About this time I also remembered a large gray boulder below the tree trunk where Phoebe and I had often sat. Just for a moment my courage failed me.

"Nothing venture, nothing have," I reminded myself. It was a favorite motto of Captain Preble's and I repeated it several times as I made ready. "After all, it isn't as if I were made of ordinary wood."

Up went my feet, out went my arms, and PLOP!

It would have been easier if I could have let go by degrees, if I could have put first one arm and then a leg over, but the nature of my pegging forbade this. My legs and arms must move together or not at all.

"Caw, caw, caw!"

I heard the Mother Crow coming and knew there was not a moment to lose. Fortunately for me, the young crows heard this, too, and began flinging themselves about the nest so violently that I could not have stayed in if I had wanted. Up went my two feet, out went my arms, and *plop!* I dropped over the edge!

The darkness seemed like a bottomless pit into which I was falling. Stiff pine needles and cones scratched my face and sharp twigs tore at me as I fell—down, down, down. I do not believe that falling from the moon itself would have seemed any farther to me. By the time I stopped I thought I must certainly have reached the bottom. Still, I felt pine needles and branches about me and when I stretched out my arms there was no comforting solid earth between them.

But the new position in which I found myself when morning came was little better than my old one. Instead of falling clear of the old pine, as I had expected, I had become entangled in one of the outer branches. There I dangled ignominiously in midair with my head down and my petticoats over it. My discomfort was great, but it was nothing compared to the humiliation I felt at this unladylike attitude, which I could do nothing to change. Indeed, I could scarcely move at all, so firmly was I caught.

And now an even more trying experience awaited me. I soon discovered that although I could see plainly everything that went on about the Preble house, I might have been a pine cone for all the notice I got. The pine tree was tall and bare of branches halfway up the trunk. It never occurred to one of the family to stand underneath and look for me in such a place. So I hung there for a number of days and nights, headfirst, drenched by rains and buffeted by every wind that blew by. But the greatest hardship of all was when I must see Phoebe Preble moving about below me, sitting on the boulder directly beneath my branch so that its very shadow fell on her curls, and yet be unable to make her look up.

"Suppose," I thought sadly, "I have to hang here till my clothes fall into tatters. Suppose they never find me till Phoebe is grown up and too old for dolls."

I know she missed me. I heard her tell Andy so, and he promised to go once more with her to look for me in the raspberry patch. They were sure the Indians had carried me away and I think this made Phoebe even more distressed about my loss. And all the time I hung just overhead with my skirts turned down till I must have looked like an umbrella inside out.

Curiously enough, it was the crows who were the means of reuniting us in the end. During the days immediately following my departure from their nest they had begun to try their own wings. Such flappings and cawing as they made, too. Never have I heard anything like it since, but then I never knew any other crows so intimately as those. Mrs. Preble said their goings-on were driving her distracted, and Andy spent most of his time aiming at them with pebbles and a sling shot. He never by any chance hit one, but they cawed as if he had. Finally, one morning when he stood right under the old pine with his sling shot all poised and ready, he caught sight of me. I suppose the yellow of my dress attracted his attention, but even then it was some time before he made out what I was.

"Phoebe!" he screamed, when he suddenly realized his find, "come and see what's growin' on the old pine."

He dropped his sling shot and ran to fetch her. Soon the whole family were all gathered in a group under me discussing the best way to bring me back to earth. It was a very serious problem, for the tree trunk was enormous and even if Captain Preble lifted Andy on his shoulders there was not a single branch for him to climb by. No ladder was long enough to reach me, and as I hung far out toward the tip, it looked as if the only way would be to cut down the whole tree. This Mrs. Preble steadily refused to consider. She said it was an ancestral pine and belonged to the family as much as the brass door-knocker or the pine dresser. Andy tried shying green apples, but I was hooked too firmly for these to dislodge me and they dared not use stones. I began to feel desperate.

Then Captain Preble, who had been gone some time, reappeared with a long birch pole he had cut. This was tall enough to reach me, but though both he and Andy worked for over an hour they could not bring me down, for no matter how sharply they whittled the end of the wood, I was too firmly hooked to be dislodged. At last, Phoebe's mother appeared at the kitchen door with a long frying fork in one hand and a plate of fresh doughnuts in the other. That gave the Captain an idea.

"Just you let me try lashin' that fork on here," he said, " and we'll grapple for her."

Quick as a wink he had the doughnut fork tied to the

sapling. The steel prongs looked rather terrifying at such close range, but I was in no mood to be critical. I did not wince when I felt them sticking into me even more sharply than the Crow's claws. To my joy I felt myself lifted free of the pine bough.

"More'n one way to harpoon your whale!" he laughed as he put me in Phoebe's hands, "and more'n one use for a doughnut fork!" he added as he gave it back.

"I wouldn't wonder but those pesky crows fetched her 'way over here from the Back Cove," Andy told Phoebe. "It don't seem hardly possible; still, they do say they're awful thieves."

But Phoebe was too happy to have me back to bother about that or even to grieve much over the sad state of my clothes. As for me, I had no other wish than to stay in her lap forever and ever.

## CHAPTER III
# In Which I Travel—by Land and Sea

Because my clothes had suffered so much from crows, rain, and sharp twigs I was unable to be seen much in polite society. But after my late experiences I was thankful enough to stay in a neat little cradle Captain Preble had made in odd moments. Phoebe's mother had promised to cut out new garments for me as soon as she could find the time. But time was evidently very hard to find in the Preble house in those days, for the Captain was soon to sail on another long voyage. It was to be a whaling trip this time and he had bought more than half interest in the ship *Diana,* which was being repaired and fitted out in Boston.

And so it came to be September, with such a shine on sea and leaf and every grass blade that even I experienced a strange springing feeling down to my very pegs. Never since then have I heard crickets make such high and persistent chirpings. All day and all night you might hear them at it in the brown, burnt grass.

"They're singin' to keep the cold away," Andy told Phoebe one night as we three sat on the doorstep, watching the big red fall moon rise behind the seaward islands.

"And can they?" Phoebe was always very curious about such things.

"No," Andy assured her, "they only think they can. The colder it turns the louder they holler, but the frost always gets 'em. You wait an' see."

"I'm glad we're not crickets," said Phoebe, hugging me tighter, as if she feared I might turn into one.

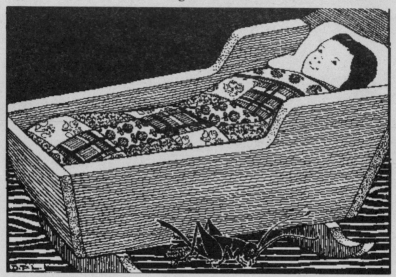

I lay in my cradle and listened to the crickets chirping.

That night after the whole house was still and everyone in bed, I lay in my cradle and listened to them and thought of what Andy had said. I, too, felt very glad I was not a cricket.

Captain Preble was forever riding over to Portland to see if the post that came by stage three times a week from Boston had brought him news of the *Diana*. There had been many delays about the ship's outfitting and the Captain was growing impatient.

"Reuben Somes is first-rate at strikin' whales," I heard him tell his wife one day, "but he's no hand at gettin' a ship overhauled. Guess I'll have to go up to Boston by the next stage-coach if we expect to weigh anchor before November. This is the last time I put in at Boston. It'll be Portland for me from now on."

"Now, Dan'l, don't you go off 'fore I get your twelfth pair o' socks knitted," his wife begged. "I couldn't rest easy here at home if I thought you was sloshin' round in wet feet!"

"Guess there's nothin' for it but to fetch you along to Boston with me day after tomorrow," he laughed. "You can finish 'em on the way and fit yourself an' Phoebe out with new winter woolens in style."

"My goodness, Dan'l, who ever heard of such nonsense?" she answered with a serious head shake. "You always were one for extravagance—two lamps burnin' an' no ship at sea!"

Her words puzzled me at the time, but I later learned that this was a phrase often used by wives of whalers and meant that some one was spending what he had not yet earned. I was to hear many such sea terms before very long.

Somehow or other the Captain always got his way. So it came about that one fine fall morning we all set off to catch the Boston stage. The sun had been up only a little while as we went clattering away, leaving the square white Preble house, the red barn, and the ancestral pine behind us. Little did I think as these familiar shapes slipped from view that I was not to see them again in another week. No, not one of us guessed, then, all that lay before us as we turned into the Portland road.

Such a morning as it was, too! I shall never forget the scarlet of the swamp maples by every pond or bit of marshy land, the bright yellow of elms and birches, and the flaming red of woodbine that made the fences look as if they had burst into flame. It was goldenrod and asters all the way to Portland.

"There, Kate," said the Captain, suddenly pointing with his whip, "that's the first mountain-ash tree I've seen this fall."

There, sure enough, at the edge of some woods was a slim, tallish tree loaded down with bunches of orange berries. The tree seemed to bend under their weight and they shone like burnished balls.

"That's Hitty's tree," cried Phoebe, "and it's magic!"

"Hush, child," reproved her mother, "you mustn't say such things."

"But the Old Peddler said so, Mother," Phoebe insisted. "Don't you remember when he was making her he said it was a charm against evil?"

"Well, now, I guess he was just givin' you a fish story," put in the Captain hastily, for he saw his wife look rather stern. "Anyhow, it's what I call a pretty sight. Geddap, Charlie, or we'll be too late for the stage."

We were in plenty of time, however. In fact, the Prebles were able to stop for doughnuts, gingerbread, and glasses of cider at Cousin Robinson's on Congress Street where Charlie and the gig were to be left while we were away.

There are no such stagecoaches nowadays, or such fine, prancing horses to draw them. This one was painted red and yellow, and the four horses were matched in pairs, two grays and two chestnuts. The spokes of the wheels were painted black and when they turned very fast it made one quite dizzy, especially if one hung out of the window and looked down. Perhaps this was the matter with Phoebe, for after we had been jolting and rumbling along for about an hour she complained of not feeling well. Captain Preble and Andy had climbed on top with several other men and boys and the driver. However, there were two or three ladies riding inside with us and they were full of sympathy and advice. One brought out peppermint lozenges, another lemon drops, and I think there were other remedies in the shape of dried licorice roots and homemade spruce beer. Phoebe tried them all. But none made her feel any better. She grew very pale and was glad to lie still with closed eyes as we rolled along at a fine pace.

"I am afraid," her mother told the other ladies with a doleful head shake, "that she must have inherited a weak stomach. It runs in our family."

I was happy to think that I was subject to no such discomfort. Though, of course, I had been unable to indulge in the cider and gingerbread at Cousin Robinson's! I suppose that may have had something to do with it.

We stayed the night at a fine old tavern in Portsmouth and were off again before daylight. Fresh horses were harnessed and the stage was soon rumbling toward Salem.

Phoebe proved herself a better traveler the second day, and her mother chatted with two new lady passengers, her needles clicking briskly as she continued to knit the Captain's socks. So past harbors and headlands, by farms and fields and elmshaded village streets we came at last to Salem. Here was a fine harbor full of ships and larger houses than I had ever seen before. We walked up and down in the early twilight. Some of the houses were of brick with small square balconies built on their roofs about the chimneys. "Captain's walks," Phoebe's father said they were called, because one could walk there and see what vessels were in the harbor. Her mother kept marveling at the size and grandeur of the homes we passed, admiring the elaborate carving over doors and windows and the handsome furnishings that we caught glimpses of within.

"They can afford it," her husband explained. "Salem's 'bout the richest port there is in these parts. If I was to take you down to the wharves, you'd see 'em loaded down with cargoes from India and China and heaven knows where. Maybe if I strike luck this voyage and bring back six or seven hundred barrels of sperm, we can come an' live here, too. How'd you like that, Kate?"

But his wife shook her head.

"You know well enough I wouldn't live anywhere except in the State of Maine. But I s'pose there's no harm in my admirin' other folks' front doors and parlor curtains, is there?"

The Captain allowed there wasn't.

By the next evening we were settled in Boston in a couple of rooms an old lady let out to sailors' families. The Captain had known her since he was a boy, and she welcomed us warmly. From her upper windows we could see the harbor with a perfect forest of masts where the vessels lay anchored near the wharves.

The Captain had gone at once to his ship, taking Andy with him. Phoebe and I were through supper and in bed by the time he returned. He sounded worried and kept repeating over and over that he should have come before and how they must get off soon if they were to make headway against the autumn gales. Some of his best men were sick or had signed up for other ships; the vessel was only half fitted out and he could not find a proper cook. This last difficulty seemed to worry him most of all. Ship's cooks were apparently scarce that year.

Several more days passed. The Captain was busier than ever down at the wharves. I had a feeling that something was going to happen, so I was not surprised when he came back one night and had a long talk with Phoebe's mother. I could not hear much of what they said, for Phoebe and I were in bed and they sat with their heads close together by the little glass lamp on the table. Captain Preble had charts spread out before him, besides a great many other papers, and his wife listened to him so intently as he talked and pointed things out to her with his big forefinger that she let her knitting lie idle in her lap.

"Well, Dan'l," she said at last, "I'll take the night to think it over and let you know by morning. I never 'lotted on going to sea, least of all to cook for a parcel of hungry men in one of these greasy old 'blubber-hunters,' as you call 'em."

"'T won't be so bad's you think," he told her, "there ain't another vessel has had so good an overhauling. You can fix your cabin up 'most as nice as if you was at home, and as for the work, why you'll have some one to do for you hand an' foot."

"But when I think of my kitchen at home," she sighed, "an' all my jelly there on the table, and our cow with the neighbors, and Charlie eatin' his head off with oats in Portland, I don't hardly feel I can."

"Don't you mind about that," he assured her.

"Well, if I do go the name of that ship's got to be changed to something more Christian." She spoke very firmly.

"They say it's bad luck to change a vessel's name," the Captain told her. "Not that I hold to that sort o' thing, but crews get notions and you have to humor 'em."

But his wife held firmly to her convictions.

"Crew or no crew," said she, "I don't set foot on any ship with such a heathen-sounding name."

So the Captain said he would see what could be done, and by breakfast time the next morning it was all settled that we should go.

Phoebe and I spent most of the day by ourselves, for the Captain and his wife were both far too busy making last purchases and seeing to all the final preparations on the eve of our departure. We were glad enough when Andy put in his appearance after supper to help a couple of big sailors carry down boxes. Andy acted very important and proud of himself in the new pea-jacket and sea boots that Captain Preble had bought him. He seemed years older than he had a week before and took his new duties as cabin-boy very seriously. I did not think he sounded particularly pleased to have us going along.

"They all say a vessel's no place for women folks," he explained to us, "and they don't want you to go only for the pie and doughnuts."

"Well, I don't care what they say," Phoebe told him with an emphatic shake of her curls, "we're going. Father said so this morning and he's Captain."

It was well after sunset by the time we went down to the wharves, but we could make out the dark outlines of hulls and masts and the shapes of men and piled-up cargoes in the flickering light of lanterns and the thin fall dusk.

"There she is," said the Captain suddenly, pointing to a looming shape alongside of the wharf. "That's your new home, Phoebe. Reckon you're goin' to like it?"

We were swung aboard like so many parcels. High overhead the masthead lantern gleamed whitely in a circle of paler light it sent out into the darkness. Below us, strapped into a little sling of a seat, a man was whistling as he moved a big brush to and fro.

Captain Preble beckoned us over to watch him.

"There's Jim," he said to his wife, "followin' your orders." Then as she looked at him blankly he smiled and explained: "He's paintin' new letters to her name—she's goin' to be the *Diana-Kate* from now on. Guess you an' that old heathen lady goddess might's well get used to each other, for you're goin' to have about eleven months of keepin' close company there astern."

And so our voyage began.

## CHAPTER IV
# In Which We Go to Sea

That night Phoebe and I spent on a horsehair sofa of extraordinary slipperiness in the aftercabin of the *Diana-Kate.* Later, Phoebe was to have a berth fitted for her in the Captain's quarters, but our coming had been so unexpected there was time for nothing besides getting the vessel in readiness to weigh anchor.

"I aim to put out by four," I heard Captain Preble telling the man that Andy had called the mate, "and we'll make the tide serve us out."

I remember his words distinctly, for I considered it very obliging of the tide to be willing to serve us. It amazes me to think how ignorant I was then of the simplest sea phrases.

All that night as Phoebe and I slid and slipped on the horsehair, I listened to the strange sounds which were to become familiar to me for many months. Such rattlings and squeakings, and such grinding of chains and clumping of boots on the wooden decks overhead. There were cries, as well, that I could not make out. It was all very enlivening.

When Phoebe carried me up the steep steps of the companionway and on deck next morning, we found the *Diana-Kate* running before the wind. Her square sails were billowing out in fine fashion and her bow dipped and rose to be lifted by great blue-green combers the like of which I had never seen before.

"Huh, this ain't nothin'," Andy told us, as Phoebe nearly lost her footing when the deck suddenly seemed to slip from under her, "you just wait till we get 'round by ol' Hatt'ras an' then you'll see somethin'."

"A lot you know 'bout Hatt'ras, young man," said a deep voice nearby, and a big man in faded blue trousers and shirt stopped beside us, "you run along down to the galley and help same's you're here for. Scud now."

Andy scudded as he was told. He disappeared down the stairs we had just climbed and presently the smell of coffee began to mingle with the sea air. The big sailor lifted Phoebe to a seat on a carpenter's wooden bench. This stood amidships near what I later learned were the try-works but which then looked to me only like deep pits of brick built into the deck between the masts. Several men were working nearby at odd jobs. They were all brown and big like the first.

"Well, so we've got ladies aboard this trip, eh, Bill?" one greeted us, giving Phoebe a knowing wink as he made the most intricate knottings of rope between his fingers. "S'pose that means we'll have to mind our P's and Q's."

Phoebe was being measured for the new bunk she was to sleep in and I for a little rope hammock which the sailor named Elija, called 'Lige for short, had promised to make me. They were so jolly and friendly and the strong sea sunshine felt so good, with the wind blowing and the big ballooning sails throwing shadows on each other, that I felt only pleasure as I looked out upon the miles of tossing blue water before us— not a single regret to see the far hump of land that was Boston disappearing from sight.

Phoebe was only a little seasick those first days out, the rest of us not at all. Andy sang and whistled and danced hornpipes the crew taught him. Even Mrs. Preble grew more resigned to the cramped quarters of the ship's galley and made a batch of molasses cookies big enough for all, a rare treat indeed for a whaling ship, or for any vessel, in those days.

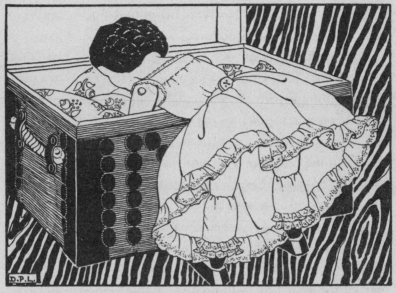

He made me a sea chest to hold my possessions.

Although there were still one or two who grumbled and made dire predictions about the presence of women aboard a whaler, we were for the most part treated with real consideration. In fact, Phoebe Preble and I were soon on such friendly terms with various members of the crew that her mother complained there would be no living with the child when we got home again. I, too, felt a distinct sense of my own importance when 'Lige and his special crony, one Reuben Somes, said that they had no doubt I would bring them good luck on this voyage. They decided this after Phoebe had told them the story of my being made of mountain-ash wood.

"Why, now, she'd ought to be as much good to us as old lady Diana down yonder," Reuben said, pointing toward the carved figurehead just under the bowsprit.

I must confess that I felt a little frightened lest he should suggest that I too be nailed in a like position, to be drenched in salt spray whenever the vessel took any particularly big wave. I did not envy the poor lady. I was far too grateful for all my privileges, especially for the little hammock 'Lige had made me. I had other presents as well, for the men all seemed to be clever at making things from odds and ends of rope, chips, or bits of wood. They vied with one another at fitting me out, and before we were many weeks out I possessed not only a hammock to sleep in but also a chip basket, a carved bone footstool, and a sea chest to hold all my possessions. This last was the gift of Bill Buckle, who spared no pains to make it perfect in every respect. It was painted a beautiful bright blue, with proper rope handles at each end and my initials, H. P., picked out in shiny nail heads on the lid. That was a proud day for me, and Phoebe was so pleased she ran all over the ship exhibiting it. She was all for climbing up to the crow's nest to show the lookout, but her father soon put a stop to that.

And this reminds me, I was greatly upset the first time I heard mention of the crow's nest. Naturally, my own trying experiences in the old pine were still fresh in my memory and I had no desire to repeat them. However, I soon discovered my mistake and later on it became one of my greatest diversions to watch the men climb up the ratlines to take their turns at watching for whales from that little black perch so high above the rigging. But I am getting a trifle ahead of myself, for it was not until we were well past the Horn and heading into the South Seas that our whaling adventures began in earnest.

The weather was generally so mild and fine, the winds so brisk and steady, that we made excellent runs during our first months out. Different seamen as well as Andy took turns at helping Mrs. Preble in the little galley that served as kitchen, "tending the kettle halyards," they called it in their own particular sea talk. She was growing used to the ship and when things had been going their best she was heard to declare that except for the lack of a few neighbors to drop in of an evening, and a decent sink for washing dishes, and a cow to give us milk, she could think of a lot worse places to spend one's days in. There were, of course, other times, such as Sundays, when she sighed remembering how many miles lay between us and Meeting-House Hill. Then she would call Andy and Phoebe to her to make sure that they had not forgotten the Commandments and the Twenty-Third Psalm.

Bill Buckle was now our constant companion and we were on such intimate terms with him that he even went as far as to loan Andy his jackknife and showed us all his best tattoo marks. Nearly all the men aboard were tattooed, but none could show such elaborate decorations as his, for there were mermaids and sea serpents in green on one arm, an anchor and whale in blue on the other, while a clipper ship in full rig and three colors was sailing straight across his chest. Andy was very envious of these pictures, but it was rather discouraging to find how much Bill Buckle had paid to have them done. He did agree, however, to tattoo Andy's initials across his chest the first chance he got. Phoebe felt a trifle left out when she heard this and was all for having mine done, too. This frightened me considerably and I was thankful enough when Bill came to my rescue by declaring that he didn't hold with tattooing for ladies. Kind Bill Buckle, I can see his great brown fingers now, his bristling black beard, and his eyes that squinted into pale blue slits when he looked far off to sea.

Another great favorite of ours was Jeremy Folger from Nantucket. He had had a fall from a yardarm in his youth, so he told us, and this had given him a hump on his back for life. It made him cut a queer figure but in no way unfitted him for ship's duties. In fact, Captain Preble counted himself lucky to have Jeremy aboard this trip, for he was known to be one of the best harpooners anywhere about. He had the keenest eyes as well as the steadiest aim. There was a rumor, which Andy and Phoebe firmly believed, that he could sight a whale spouting, or rather blowing, as they called it, fully nine miles away. He had no beard like the rest and his straw-colored hair was bleached almost white by the strong sea sunshine. This gave him the oddest appearance. To this day I do not know whether he was nearer twenty or seventy.

One night I heard Captain Preble tell his wife the only thing that bothered him was that "everything was *drawing* 'most too well." Just when that was it is difficult to remember, for there was little to separate one long, blue, salty day from the one that came before or after it. However, soon after we had come around that mysterious place they all called the Horn, the *Diana-Kate* struck a spell of bad weather. The storm came on quite suddenly late one afternoon and there was barely time to get canvas lashed and hatches battened down before we were in the teeth of it. No more sunny hours of leisure and yarn-spinning on deck, but two days and nights of pounding, tossing, and buffetings such as no pen can describe. The rocking and roaring about the nest in the old pine were as nothing to what I now experienced.

"Now don't you go and get wadgetty, Kate," Captain Preble told his wife, as he took a final look about the cabin to make sure all was tight before going on deck. "It won't be exactly smooth sailin' for a spell, but I've put through worse'n this is goin' to be. I mean to heave to and lay under bare poles till this is over with."

"Well, put on an extra pair of socks, Dan'l, an' take your muffler aloft," was all she said, but I could see that she was worried.

"What did he mean about layin' under bare poles?" Phoebe asked curiously.

"Means he don't dast have an inch of sail up," Andy told her. "Guess I'll go above an' have a look around."

"You won't do any such thing," Mrs. Preble spoke up briskly. "It's all the men can do to keep their footing on desk; you'd be washed overboard in no time. You come right in the galley with me and help get the fire goin' and some hot soup ready. Dear knows they'll need it tonight if they never did before."

Although it was long before the time, Phoebe and I were put to bed in her little bunk and tied in firmly with an old piece of flannel.

"Can't have you fallin' down and breakin' your bones," her mother said when she protested. "We've got trouble enough on our hands as 'tis."

So in bed we stayed, though it was impossible to sleep in all the racket going on about us. A single oil lamp hung in the main cabin just outside. This was the only light, dim and rather smoky at best, and now, with the ship reeling and plunging with such violence, it swung crazily about, making eerie shadows that frightened Phoebe into tears. But since no one heard her above the commotion, and if they had all were too busy to stop and reassure her, she finally ducked her head under the blankets and held me close.

"Oh, Hitty," she whispered, "I didn't think going to sea would be like this, did you?"

It seemed as if that night would never turn into morning, and when it did we were no better off, for it was almost as dark and noisy below as at midnight. To add to our discomfort, water poured down whenever the hatchway was opened, and even when it was not, it managed to seep in as often as a particularly huge wave broke over the *Diana-Kate's* bow and made her decks awash with tons of salt water. Already there were several inches on the cabin floor, and Mrs. Preble was in despair, trying to keep the fire alive.

"You'd best stay in your bunk same's Phoebe," the Captain told her on one of his few trips below. "I'd send one of the crew down to help you, but the truth is I can't spare a one of 'em. She's sprung a leak for'ard and it takes four to keep her bailed out."

"Mercy, Dan'l!" I heard Mrs. Preble cry out. "Ain't that pretty bad?"

"Well, I can't say it's exactly good," he answered as he stood by the cabin door gulping down some hot tea she had brought him in a tin cup. "Trouble is we can't commence patchin' till this lets up. But it's bound to 'fore long, if we can just ride it out."

How that day passed I do not know. All I remember of it is the absolute certainty that the *Diana-Kate's* next downward plunge would surely send us to the bottom. Whenever she rose, shuddering and straining in every beam, I felt it must be for the last time, and then once more we would begin to sink down, down, till it seemed impossible we could ever again climb out of such a watery hollow.

The noise grew to be so great that even the men's shrillest shouts to one another could scarcely be heard above the sloshings and poundings, the thud and crash of waves breaking over and about us, and the wind that howled and tore at masts till it seemed they must crack in two. Indeed, during that second night of storm it increased with such violence that the accident occurred which was so nearly our finish.

By this time, what with the leak we had sprung and the force of the waves breaking over our bows, the foc's'le was partly under water. Those of the crew who ordinarily slept there must snatch the few winks of sleep allowed them in the cabin. Not that any part of the ship was dry now, but they were too wet from their struggles overhead to notice a few inches of water underfoot. Once or twice we caught sight of Jeremy or Bill Buckle or other special cronies, who were too spent and dripping to give us more than a nod or grin. It was no time for pleasantry, I can tell you.

Several of the men were gathered there trying to wring some of the wet from their soaked jackets when there came a particularly strong gust of wind. We could feel the *Diana-Kate* shiver under the force of it; and then came a sound of such horrid ripping and splintering that it makes me terrified to think of it even now in the quiet of the antique shop. There followed a noise of hurrying feet on deck, more cracking, and Captain Preble bellowing out commands in a voice that sounded no bigger than a cricket chirping above the tumult.

"Cut her away, boys!" he was shouting. "Let her go—topsail an' all!"

I saw the three men who had been lounging in the cabin leap to their feet and go staggering up the companionway. Even in the wavering light of the oil lamp I could make out how pale Phoebe's mother had grown as she started up from her place in the bunk below us. She clung to the child with one hand, while with the other she kept herself from falling.

"What's happened, Mother? Are we going to sink?" Phoebe cried, seeing the fright in her face.

"Not if your father can help it," her mother answered, but her eyes were enormous and she never even noticed that she was standing in water to her ankles.

"I don't believe we will—not with Hitty aboard," Phoebe reminded her. "She's made of mountain-ash wood and you know that's sure to bring us good luck."

But Mrs. Preble was too anxious to hear or reprove her.

After what seemed a long time things quieted down somewhat above us. The men returned to the cabin and the Captain came down for a moment to reassure his wife. From him we learned that the main topmast had snapped in two and it had been necessary for several of the crew to climb up and cut it away, topsail, yardarm, and dear knows how much besides.

"Yes," he said, shaking the wet from his beard and eyebrows, "it's gone over the side and lucky we didn't follow it."

"Oh, Dan'l," his wife cried out, "can't you let me get you a dry shirt?"

But he was gone before she could make her way over to the chest.

Later on, Andy visited us. He had been with the men in the cabin and so had gathered much news about our situation. He crawled into our bunk and sat cross-legged at the foot while he regaled Phoebe with all he had learned.

"They thought we were gone for good that time," he told us. "Bill Buckle said it looked as if we were going to join the fishes in another five minutes, only for Jeremy and 'Lige cutting off the topmast and sail in such a hurry. Cap'n knew it was the only way, but old Patch is terrible mad. He was all for tryin' to save it."

Patch was the first mate, a stoop-shouldered, sandy man, who had never muttered more than a curt good morning to us since we set sail. I had never liked him and now I felt sure that he meant no good to any of us.

"He was all agin havin' women folks along," Andy went on. "They say he done everything he could, only the Cap'n went over his head. Now he's goin' round sayin' we're gettin' our bad luck same's he said we would for havin' you aboard. Bill Buckle don't pay no heed to him, but he says there's some that does, though he ain't mentionin' names."

## CHAPTER V
# In Which We Strike Our First and Last Whales

Well, at last it turned smooth and blue again, bluer than I have ever seen water before or since. We were in the South Seas now, heading for what the men all agreed was the best whaling ground, though what ground there was about these miles of sea I could not make out. The *Diana-Kate* seemed to be almost herself again after the accident she had suffered in the storm. Her leak had been patched, a new topsail and mast concocted. The long boats were repainted and given thorough overhaulings, irons greased, harpoons sharpened, and ropes tarred in readiness for the first cry from the lookout that he saw a whale coming up to blow.

It was about this time that Phoebe Preble, as well as the ship, underwent some overhauling. As the weather had grown hotter and hotter she had discarded her woolens. But this was not enough. One by one, she shed first her merino dress, then her knitted stockings, then her flannel petticoats, and last of all her curls. These were removed with great ceremony in the presence of nearly all the crew, who gathered about the barrel on which she sat to make sure the job was properly done. 'Lige, who did all such services aboard ship, was as thorough with his scissors as with his other tools, and when he had finished, Phoebe's mother almost cried.

"This is what comes of taking her to sea," she lamented. "You wouldn't know her for the same child we fetched aboard."

Her father could not very well deny this, what with the freckles and tan she had acquired into the bargain. But he only laughed at his wife's head-shakings.

"Better have it off 'n full of whale oil," he told her. "All she needs now is a pair of breeches. Guess I'll get Jim to cut down those old nankeens of Andy's. We won't be making a port for months, so who cares how she looks?"

So breeches it was, despite all her mother's protests.

I must confess to having some misgivings when I saw her in them, lest she might have changed in her feelings for dolls. But she was as devoted to me as ever. I went with her everywhere and that is how I came to be upon such familiar terms with whales, an advantage such as few dolls can boast. Now as I sit in the antique shop and look up at the whaling print hanging over the desk, it seems strange to me that I can remember just such scenes. First there would be the thrilling cry from the lookout aloft: "There she blows!" or, more often, just "Blow—o—ows!" Then the *Diana-Kate* would become all a-bustle. Our course must be changed to bring us as near as possible to where the pale jet of water, which the whale sent up like a fountain, had been last sighted. Meantime the longboats would be made ready to swing out at the order from Captain Preble to "lower an' fetch him." Sometimes five boats put out for the chase, more often three, the men bending briskly to their oars, as they sped toward that dark-gray mound that looked as big as Huckleberry Hill at home and yet disappeared as suddenly as it had come, to rise again at an entirely different spot.

Jeremy Folger was the first to "strike" a whale, but no one begrudged him the glory, for he had to drive more than one iron into the great creature and was himself all but swept into the sea when the whale became gallied and nearly upset the long boat. It was a sperm whale of extraordinary size, such as any captain and crew might covet. All the men received shares of the oil, and so they were determined not to let such a prize escape. With Phoebe and Andy I watched the boats lowered and saw them speed away, each leaving a white trail behind. There were five rowers in each of the three and their oar blades moved like one as they pulled away from us in the strong sea sunshine.

"Greasy luck, boys!" called Captain Preble as he watched them go.

How should I, a little wooden doll, be able to tell of such things—of those boats that looked no bigger than pea pods currying through the water toward that enormous gray shape that appeared and disappeared so mysteriously, sending its ghostly stream of water high in air? I cannot believe that I did actually see this for myself, and yet I know that it was so. Indeed, as luck would have it, the whale made such a wide circle in its fight that it brought up near enough for us to see much of the chase. Andy pressed close to the low rail, shading his eyes with his hands as he strained to make out the figures in the long-boats.

"There 'tis!" he cried, so shrilly Phoebe almost dropped me over the side in her excitement to follow his pointing forefinger. "It's white-waterin' again. See it spout! Jeremy's boat's ahead. I can tell his red 'n' white shirt."

"Where?" Phoebe hopped up and down beside him, holding me close.

"Why, there, in the bow. Watch now, he's goin' to strike in a minute!"

The oars suddenly hung poised in midair and the little slip of a boat seemed about to vanish under the glistening dark mass above it.

In that second of time I suddenly had a sickening recollection of the picture in the illustrated Bible I had been forced to see during my stay under the Preble pew. Somehow I had not before connected that great sea creature with the whales we were to capture. Now I knew that they were one and the same and I seemed to see poor Jeremy instead of the man in the picture being swallowed up in that awful abyss.

But next thing I knew Andy was screaming out jubilantly that Jeremy had "struck his whale."

"Now they're off for a Nantucket sleigh-ride," he told Phoebe. "That's what they call it," he explained, "when the harpoon's in fast and they can just pay out the rope an' follow him round."

"But I don't see the whale anywhere now," protested Phoebe.

"He'll be up again pretty quick," Andy assured her, "he can't get very far the way they've got him hooked."

It was certainly the truth. Presently the dark shape rose from the water again, struggling and plunging this time, trying to shake himself free. His great sides showed sleek and glittering in the sun, more water spouted into the air, and the sea was churned white and swirling by the gigantic lashings of his tail. How long he dragged the boat after him, or how many times he plunged under water to reappear again with more furious wallowings, I do not know. At last, however, there were streaks of red mixed with the white foam. A cry went up from watchers aboard the *Diana-Kate*.

"Whale's gallied. It'll be fin-out soon."

Sure enough, before many more minutes the lashings grew less frequent, then they ceased altogether. The whale's great body rose a little more out of the water, then turned over slowly till a sharp black fin showed plainly. There came another shout from those on deck and still more from those in the boats.

"Well, we got him," said Captain Preble with satisfaction, as he turned to his wife. "Think maybe you could fix up somethin' extra in the grub line to celebrate?"

Next day the cutting-in began and I was to know the whale still more intimately. Even after all these years I can remember how it looked stretched out at full length alongside of the ship. By the time Phoebe brought me on deck the morning after our first chase, the men were lowering a little platform upon which they stood with long hooks, knives, and other implements that looked altogether too sharp to please me. With ropes and various lines they managed to hoist the whale up, meantime having begun cutting it in such a manner that the blubber peeled off in long strips as neatly as if it had been an apple. But apple it was not as we very soon discovered once it was aboard and in the try-works. I began to wonder how there would be any whale-oil left to be stored in the casks, so much of it ran over the decks. The whole ship reeked of it. But no one paid any attention to this except Mrs. Preble, who said she had never in all her days smelled such a smell or seen such a mess of the grease. The men only laughed and said this was "greasy luck!" They went their different ways—some to toil at the hoisting and cutting, others to mince the hunks of blubber into pieces for the try-pots, and still others to skim off the scraps that kept the fires going night and day.

Thick black smoke rose and hung over us amidships like a queer umbrella, while at night the light of the fires made a dull red glow. This added to the heat and oiliness aboard. The men worked continuously with only a few hours off for rest.

"Got to push it through so's we can go after another," Captain Preble explained, as he came to eat his supper a few nights later, his hands so stiff from the work of cutting-in that he could scarcely hold his knife and fork.

Even Andy was pressed into service mincing and carrying. He went about very proudly, stripped to the waist like the rest, his trousers rolled to his knees. Sometimes his face was so black from oil and smoke that his blue eyes looked very strange in the midst of it and his red hair topping it even stranger. Phoebe and I were not allowed to venture very near the try-works. Her father had been firm about this.

"Can't have you gettin' underfoot an' maybe scalded," he told her.

So it came about that we took our place on an old barrelhead some yards away, but near enough to watch much of the work. I was relieved we were no nearer, for I had no desire to find myself swimming in the boiling try-pots and I might easily have slipped in along with a piece of blubber.

Scarcely was one whale turned into oil before they would be off for another, and indeed, on one occasion, when a whole school of them was sighted, they took several and towed them back to the ship. It was strange to see these enormous gray bulks anchored nearby with small flags fastened to our irons to show they were our property. By this time a couple of other whaling vessels had arrived in the grounds. There was considerable rivalry among them, even though we were several miles from one another. There was talk among the men about going "gamming." One never hears that word nowadays, but then it was common enough among seafaring people. It meant paying social visits from one ship to another while at sea. All the men were anxious to do this, but Captain Preble decided that the cutting-in must be finished first. There was some grumbling over this, and some very black looks on the part of Patch, who evidently began to feel he was first in command instead of second. In his time off duty he was often to be found deep in conversation with some of the men, and from his expression I felt that no good would come of it.

It was unfortunate, therefore, that the ship we had intended signaling should sail away without hailing us before the last whale we had taken was more than a third minced and in the try-works. Words passed between the Captain and his first mate over this and before long the whole ship was divided as to which was in the right. Patch held that the men had a right to ask for leave to go gamming, while those who sided with the Captain maintained that to call a halt in the work would be to lose not only time but also perhaps considerable blubber and so in the end affect their shares of the oil. The Captain went about his duties quietly as if nothing had occurred out of the ordinary, but down in their cabin late at night I heard him talking it over with his wife.

"It's the last trip I take Patch on as mate," he told her. "He come to me so well recommended I thought I was lucky to have him along, especially with his taking on more shares in the vessel than any of the others who applied, but he's been makin' a regular nuisance of himself lately."

"Well, I ain't surprised, Dan'l," Mrs. Preble remarked. "I thought right from the start he had the meanest, shiftiest eye I ever did see. But 't wa'n't my place to pick your men."

"He's able enough," the Captain went on. "I couldn't honestly say he don't know the ropes or steer a straight course, but all I know is I'll feel pretty glad when we've struck our last whale and the casks are filled and we're headin' for the home port."

"Glad is nothin' to what I'll feel," his wife returned with a sigh.

But no one would have guessed from the Captain's manner on deck how he felt about things when he was below in his own cabin.

Mrs. Preble did her best in the galley. She scraped the sugar and molasses barrels clean to keep up a supply of cookies and gingerbread and stood ready and willing to fry up any messes of fresh fish the men might catch. Finally, however, our last finest sperm whale was taken. All the boats had put out after it and two reached it almost at the identical moment. There was some confusion, and orders from those in command of each boat were not followed. At least this was the story we heard afterward on board the *Diana-Kate*. At all events, there was an argument as to which had struck it first, Jeremy's harpoon, or another's. Since an extra share of the oil was allowed the one whose iron first fastened itself in the whale, the men began to take sides among themselves. They neglected their work to discuss and argue, and when Captain Preble was heard to declare that neither should benefit, their dissatisfaction grew.

Still, unpleasant as this was, none of us dreamed of the danger so shortly to threaten all our lives, least of all I who had come to feel almost secure upon this world of wood and canvas as I had in the Preble farmhouse.

I think it must have been round midnight; it was still dark, at any rate, when there came a sharp cry on deck and the quick thud of bare feet hurrying above us. Almost immediately after, we heard the call: "All hands on deck." That meant something out of the ordinary was happening, though what it might be on such a calm night in the tropic seas I could not imagine. Phoebe woke up and was all for going above, but her mother said no, they would only get in the men's way. Her father would come down to them when he could. So we three waited breathlessly in the hot, close-pressing darkness.

Then Captain Preble was at the door, his eyes red and watering.

"Dan'l, what's the matter?" cried his wife.

"The ship's afire," he told her as quietly as he could. "Must have got started down in the blubber room, the Lord knows how. I'm afraid it's spreadin', but we're doin' all we can to fight it."

"How is it now?"

"Midships and for'ard. 'T won't reach here for a good while yet. We're lowerin' wet sails on the flames; sometimes that'll smother 'em, but I'm afraid it's got too much headway."

"And the vessel fairly reekin' with whale oil, too . . ." I saw Mrs. Preble cling to him suddenly as if she were no bigger than Phoebe who sat up in her bunk listening. "Oh, Dan'l, what chance have we got?"

"Well, we won't give up fightin' it 'fore we have to," he answered. "I'm not one to leave my ship till the last, but if the worst comes to the worst and we do have to take to the boats we'll make out. It's better round here than some places we could have selected. So don't you go and get gallied, Kate."

"Who says I'm goin' to?" She was her old self again. "Phoebe 'n' I'll be ready when you need us."

"Better get some things together," he cautioned her, "what you and Phoebe might need, in case—" he broke off abruptly and turned toward the door. Even in the dim light I could see how haggard and pale his face showed under his tan and the smudges of smoke. But he squared his shoulders and went above. Presently we heard his voice bellowing orders and the scurrying of feet obeying them.

Phoebe and her mother began to get into their clothes and were soon busy collecting their belongings. Mrs. Preble moved steadily to and fro from the two chests to the bunk, where she tied and retied her things into tight bundles. Phoebe, following her mother's example, collected all my things, the blue chest, the carved footstool, and my little hammock, and put them into a splint basket. After that she dressed me and laid me in beside them. She kept asking innumerable questions: did her mother think the ship would burn up soon? Would there be room for them all in the boats? Where would they go if they left the ship? Did her mother think the men had set the blubber room afire on purpose? To all of which Mrs. Preble had to answer that she knew no more than Phoebe.

Presently Andy came down to our cabin. But he had no progress to report. In spite of all they could do, the fire was gaining on them. The wet canvas they lowered on it only made a dense, choking smoke before the flames burst out in new places.

"They all say we ain't got a chance to save her," he announced. "It's just a question of how long we can stay aboard and steer her to the best place for bein' picked up. Old Patch he thinks he knows more 'n the Captain 'bout it, an' some of the men are takin' his side."

Mrs. Preble listened to him in silence. Then she began to gather up her things.

"You take this bundle," she told him, "and come along with me. Here, Phoebe, take your things, too; if there's any trouble I don't aim to stay cooped up down here."

We found most of the crew gathered about Captain Preble and Patch, who stood arguing by the deck house with charts and maps in their hands. We waited at the top of the companionway and listened to them. Phoebe held my basket on her arm, so I had a good view of sea and sky and the familiar figures before us. A faint pink was coming into the sky, but the large tropic stars still showed pale and clear. Some of those nearest the horizon made little trails of brightness on the water, which was so smooth that the *Diana-Kate* scarcely moved at all. There was no wind to speak of, the sails barely stirred above us. We could not actually see the flames, for the smothering canvases were still down, but gray rolls of smoke curled up from between the boards and poured out in the region of the try-works. It was thick, heavy smoke that made people's eyes water and choked in their throats. Once again I found it a decided advantage to be made of wood.

I cannot recall much of what passed between the two men. Indeed, many of their words meant nothing to me, though even I could tell from their looks and tones that they were in violent disagreement. It was evident that the ship must be abandoned sooner or later; the important question had now become how to steer her remaining course so that we would find ourselves in the most likely position to be rescued by the next passing ship. The mate was set upon one direction, and Captain Preble was equally determined on the opposite one. Nearly all the crew seemed to side with Patch, insisting that since the situation had become so desperate they had a right to take matters in their own hands and save themselves as best they could. Captain Preble was not one to give in easily. Besides, he felt strongly that there were more chances of rescue by remaining aboard the ship as long as possible and then making for some islands he found charted. But Patch claimed his islands were better. He grew more excited every moment and swore the Captain's plan was as good as murder and he would not stand by and be party to it. There were mutterings and ugly looks and it soon became clear that feeling ran too high to be overcome. Several of the men refused to go aloft or take the Captain's orders. Time was passing that should have been used to good advantage, and still the smoke curled up, blacker and heavier each time I looked. Andy complained that the deck scorched his bare feet, and Mrs. Preble kept tight hold of Phoebe's hand, though she never took her eyes away from her husband's face.

Suddenly I saw him fold the chart he had been holding. Very quietly he put it into his breast pocket before he turned to Patch again.

"Steer your own course, then," he said in a voice that was so strange I hardly knew it for his. "Take the long-boats and put off, the whole plagued lot of you. I'd rather go to the bottom, me and mine, than bicker with such a comp'ny of good-for-nothing landlubbers. Take the long-boats and go, I tell you, and it can't be too soon to suit me!"

"Oh, Dan'l," I heard his wife whisper under her breath, "what have you gone an' done?"

But she made no outcry and stood quietly in her place watching Patch and the men hurry off to lower the boats.

"Stay here by me, Kate." I heard the Captain issuing commands as if his family had been some of the crew. "You, too, Andy and Phoebe, an' you're not to move, no matter what."

We stood together in a little group by the deck house, as the men ran to and fro about us. But not all, for Jeremy, Reuben, and Bill Buckle had taken their places by Captain Preble.

"We're with you, sir," they had said. "We'll stand by as long's the ship can hold her beams together."

The sun came up out of the sea in a fiery ball and was well up in the heavens by the time the five boats were lowered. But this time there were no cheery calls from those aboard, no answering shouts. We watched them pull away in silence and I saw Mrs. Preble's lips tremble as Phoebe's might just before she began to cry. They had hoisted small canvas sails in each boat and as they moved off over the water they looked like white triangles of paper against the blue.

I shall never forget that sight, or the steady grimness with which the men pulled away, with hardly a backward look. Such kindly, pleasant friends many of them had been to us, too. I have often wondered what became of them—if they fared any better than we, or if, as the Captain believed, they steered a course to certain disaster.

It would be impossible for any pen, least of all one held in the hand of a doll, to describe our next few hours or tell how we waited under a sort of makeshift canvas tent the men hoisted astern in order that we might be protected from the heat and smoke which rapidly spread to every part of the vessel. Meantime, those three and the Captain put all their strength and skill together in a desperate effort to sail us within sight of the group of islands the Captain knew must lie somewhere to the southwest. To keep a burning ship afloat, not to speak of maneuvering it in the right direction, is not exactly an easy undertaking. Captain Preble and the three kept at it as long as possible, but finally even they gave in.

"Well, Kate, get yourself and Phoebe ready," the Captain said at last, his face streaked with smoke and sweat. "We've got the stern boats yet, and Bill's below gettin' what food an' water they've left us."

A rope ladder had been let down. It swayed giddily as Jeremy clambered up and over the side.

"Mercy!" cried Phoebe's mother in dismay, "I'll never be able to go down that."

It seemed for a minute as if she were more afraid of this than the fire. She looked more hopefully toward the boat that had not yet been lowered. But Jeremy explained that she would be more comfortable in the larger of the two.

"You hold right on to me, ma'am," he told her. "I'll give you a hand over the rail. Hoist your petticoats right up and don't stand on no ceremony."

The Captain now appeared to add his encouragement. So over the side she went, hand over hand, with Jeremy going first in case she should let go.

Andy and Bill Buckle now came up with some kegs of food and water to add to those already on the boats. Captain Preble had his smaller compass, a lantern, some instruments, and the log book. He looked more grave than I had ever seen him. A smear of smoke ran like a dark scar across one cheek, his eyes were red and swollen.

"Bill," he said, giving his last orders, "you 'n' Jeremy take Andy with you an' the extra stuff there in the other boat. Reuben and I'll look out for the women folks." Even in the midst of such danger I could not but be pleased to hear myself and Phoebe put in the same class with Mrs. Preble. "Keep your boat as close to ours as you can," he cautioned. "If I'm right in my reckoning we'd ought to sight one of the group 'fore dark."

During this conversation Phoebe had set me down in the basket on top of one of the large wooden kegs of salt meat, while she went to look for a piece of carved whalebone she had dropped. Her father, evidently fearing she might venture too near the danger line, went after her and, picking her up in his arms, hustled her over the side to Jeremy and hence into the boat. This all happened very quickly, in the twinkling of an eye, as the saying goes, though no eyes were in the mood to do such a thing in those last moments aboard the *Diana-Kate*. I was disappointed not to go along with Phoebe but comforted myself with the knowledge that I was upon one of the provision kegs and therefore sure to be taken on the other boat. So I waited, somewhat anxiously, I must confess, while the last preparations were being made. Once I thought I heard Phoebe calling from below, but the others were either too busy lowering the second boat or making too much noise to hear her. I knew she must be asking for me, and this did not make me feel any easier.

I heard the Captain issuing more orders. Then Bill Buckle began stowing the things in the second boat. The next minute I expected my turn to come—but it never did. For just as he was about to return for my keg and another even larger, some one shouted to him from below that there was not a moment to spare. Flames, higher than the men were tall, suddenly began to shoot out on both sides of the try-works and to wrap themselves about the nearer mast. They waited for nothing after that. I watched them disappear over the side—boat, men and all—knowing that with them went my last hope of being saved.

It seemed impossible to believe that I had been abandoned to such a fate, and yet I saw the two boats pulling away together. I could even make out the different figures—Andy's blue shirt, Jeremy's checked in red and white, and Mrs. Preble with her best gray beaver bonnet on because she couldn't bear not to save it. Once I was sure I saw Phoebe point back toward the ship. I knew her gesture was meant for me and just for a moment hope stirred in me again. But the boats continued steadily on their way. Soon the smoke that still hung thick about the ship shut them from my sight. Now, indeed, did I feel that destruction was at hand, for what power can save even mountain-ash wood in the midst of a roaring furnace?

Furnace was what the *Diana-Kate* was fast becoming. The heat grew more intense every moment and now flames were climbing the rigging more swiftly than any sailor had ever been able to ascend it. Terrified as I was, I remember that I could not but note how like those bright fall trees along the Portland road the masts looked wrapped in fierce, orange flames. The roar and crackle now became almost worse than the heat. I could hear beams crashing in below and a sound that sent answering shivers down to my innermost pegs—the noise of good stout wood being destroyed. I remembered that I, too, was wood, for all that I had been given form and fashion, so how could I hope to fare better than the rest against this common enemy?

I tried to think of all the cool and pleasant things I could—of snow sparkling on the old pine in the Preble dooryard; of lilacs and apple trees in bloom; of the spire on Meeting House Hill. I thought of the blue and white china on the pantry shelves, and of the crickets chirping through those crisp fall nights. How I envied them now, for surely it must be easier to die by freezing than to be burned to a crisp. It would have been a comfort to turn over on my back so that I need not see the fire eating its way nearer and nearer, but Phoebe had settled me firmly in the basket. I could not move.

"Only a miracle can save me now," I said to myself.

I had heard someone say that once, but it did not seem likely that one would come to my aid. Why should a doll expect more than a ship? Still, I had been made of mountain-ash wood and the *Diana-Kate* had not. I know of no other way to account for what happened.

Just as it seemed the paint on my face would begin to sizzle, the ship gave a tremendous lurch. I suppose some of the underpinnings must have burned away. At any rate, she pitched over crazily on her side with such force that the keg on which I had been resting rolled completely over. Out of the basket I tumbled; out I flew under the rail and into the water as neatly as a pebble from a sling shot.

"Well," I remember thinking as I took the plunge, "at least I shall not be burned up. Water is kinder to wood than fire and I have heard that salt is a great preservative."

## CHAPTER VI
# In Which I Join the Fishes and Rejoin the Prebles

When sailors speak of dying, they say they are going to "join the fishes." I came to understand the meaning of this phrase as few before me can have done. At first, it was not so bad, for I had become entangled with some of the wreckage from the ship. Indeed, I floated about for a long time quite comfortably on a coil of rope till a particularly large wave lifted me off and rolled me over on my face. This was rather less pleasant, but I was still in no mood to be critical when I remembered my narrow escape from the flames.

Here, as I sit at my ease in the antique shop and think of those days and nights that I was tossed from wave to wave, even I find it hard to believe in my own adventures or to think that I could have known those miles of salt sea and tropic sun and stars and felt the touch of those fierce, brightly colored fishes as they came up to nibble at me. They soon gave me up, however, discovering for themselves that I was wood and not to their taste. I was in constant fear that some shark or even a whale might appear and gulp me down with a mouthful of sea water. I could still recall vividly the picture in the Bible at home, and I thought, if a man could be swallowed, how much more easily I might disappear in like manner. But once again a miraculous Providence watched over me.

I floated in the quiet waters of a rock pool.

I think I must have become too water-soaked from days of buffetings to know what went on about me or by what devious and salty ways I came to the Island. But come I did in time along with other bits of wreckage. At any rate, I knew nothing till I found myself in the quiet waters of a rock pool. This was a deep hole worn in the coral and all manner of bright seaweeds clung to the sides, trailing long, wavering fingers or tresses like green and scarlet hair in the clear water. Small, shelly creatures were moving about on busy missions of their own, and a huge, spiked starfish was twining about my ankle. But I was too spent to struggle. I cared for nothing but to lie still at last after all the batterings I had suffered. The tropic sun blazed down so fiercely that soon those parts of me which were out of water became dried and all crusted over with salt.

And then, impossible though it seems to believe, I heard voices close by. For a moment I thought I must have confused them with the cries of strange birds and the noise of the surf pounding on nearby reefs. But again they came, and this time I knew them for the familiar ones of Andy and Jeremy Folger. Now, even in my joy, a new fear struck me—suppose they should not come to the pool? Suppose I must lie there and hear them go away again without me? "Oh," I thought, "to be able to cry out to them just once. To call out aloud: 'Here, here I am. Take me back to Phoebe.'"

Well, as you have guessed, they found me, else how should I be writing my memoirs today?

Andy bore me back in triumph, and they were all so overjoyed to see me again that no one scolded him for not getting any of the crabs he had been sent to hunt.

"I declare if it ain't a miracle!" Mrs. Preble exclaimed as Phoebe took me to her heart. "Wherever did you find her, Andy?"

"Down in one of those pools 'long shore," he explained with pride, "there was some wood and stuff washed up, too; Jeremy's comin' with what he can find."

"Well, it certainly beats all," Captain Preble remarked, turning me about between his thumb and forefinger. "It takes us the better part of a day to get here, charts and rudder an' four pairs of oars, an' she gets here all by herself with no trouble at all."

"Mercy," thought I, "how little he knows about it!"

"I guess she never would have got back to me if she wasn't made of mountain-ash wood," Phoebe reminded them.

This time her mother did not rebuke her.

"I wouldn't have believed how glad I'd be to see that doll again," she said. "It kind of heartens me up some way. Makes me feel maybe this Island's not so far from all creation but what something'll come along to pick us up."

"You keep your courage right with you, ma'am," put in Bill Buckle, who was busy hacking away at some underbrush of rich, damp green. "I always said that doll would bring us luck, and I say so now. I don't care who hears me."

There was, indeed, no one besides our little party to hear him except some highly colored birds and a number of small brown animals with long tails who ran, chattering, over the branches above us. These, I later learned, were called "monkeys," and I was to see far more of them before my days on the Island were over.

"I'm afraid she won't never be what she was 'fore she took

to the water," Reuben pronounced soberly, as he looked me over. "Her clothes and complexion certainly ain't been improved any!"

"No more have ours," said Mrs. Preble with a sigh and a glance toward her bedraggled bonnet hanging from a nearby branch.

Phoebe set about repairing my clothes then and there. They dried fast in the glaring sunlight and soon I, too, was dry once more, though woefully tattered and faded. Still, when I saw how the others had fared I did not feel so badly.

The Island itself was what Captain Preble had predicted, the outermost one of a small group. Although it was scarcely more than a coral reef, still a surprising amount of vegetation grew upon it—palm trees and others I did not know; trailing vines, huge ferns, and great pinkish flowers the Captain called "hibiscus." Some of the first things they had discovered were a couple of deserted huts made of grass and leaves woven between poles and tree shoots that had been driven into the ground. This had evidently been made some time before, as the leaves were brown and worn away in many places. However, Bill Buckle and the others went to work filling in the gaps and making them tight against the sudden tropic showers which would appear while the sun was still shining brilliantly, to be over before one could take shelter. It was fortunate for us that these occurred frequently, for without them we should not have known how to get water. There seemed to be none on the Island, though the men searched the length and breadth of it. However, they were able to catch enough in the kegs to keep from going thirsty long, though they were careful not to waste a single precious drop and to wash in sea water. As to food, they managed rather well, I thought, for there were many fruits of various sorts all about, not to speak of coconuts that the monkeys were forever after. Mrs. Preble did not think much of the coconuts, but Phoebe and Andy enjoyed them hugely after such a long diet of ship's biscuits and salt meat. For almost the first time in my life I felt regretful that I could not at least taste the white milk the children drank with such relish.

Captain Preble believed that there must be natives on the other larger islands, one of which showed faintly in a distant blue line. He thought that they came sometimes to our Island for fishing or some other purpose and that the huts were shelters they had left behind from their last trip. He did not seem at all anxious to have them pay us a visit, for neither he nor the men believed they would prove friendly. These islands were almost never touched at by vessels, and the reports of those who had were far from pleasant. Every day the Captain would look through his spyglass to see if there were signs of vessels or of any activity whatsoever within his range, and the boats were kept in readiness to launch at the first topsail that should appear over the horizon.

Never shall I forget my first night there in the little grass hut, with the warm, thick darkness all about us and the strange noises. There were scents, too, the like of which I had never known anywhere. Through the gaps in the hut we could see the stars, and this seemed to give Captain Preble a sense of security as he pointed out this and that one to his wife. She got little comfort out of them, however, for she said they were all in the wrong places from where she was used to seeing them and it only made her feel farther off from home.

Considering the situation, she was not so doleful as I had expected her to be. Indeed, when I remember how she had left home with no thought of a longer journey than to Boston and with the jelly still in its glasses on the kitchen table, I could not blame her if she had spells of regret and sinkings of the heart. But she was devoted to the Captain, and his predicament gave her new spirit and resourcefulness.

"Never mind, Dan'l," I heard her tell him one day when he came up from shore with his spyglass and a rather sober expression, "'t wa' n't through your fault we've come to this. Only it seems to me if we ever do get back to the State o' Maine again I'd be so thankful I could write a psalm fit to go alongside of King David's."

"Well, I know they say folks have got to take the bitter with the sweet in this world," the Captain responded, "but I must say I can't see why I had to lose my vessel an' the biggest catch I ever made an' when I had you 'n' Phoebe aboard all to once. No, I must say there's times when the ways of Providence are beyond me."

This was the nearest to complaint that I ever heard the Captain make. Before the others he was steady and good-natured, as he had always been, even cracking jokes about their food and general appearance. These certainly did not improve as the days wore on and on. He was careful to keep up his entries in the log book, though, as he said, it was the mate's duty, not his. They had no pen and ink to write with but after experimenting with a pointed stick dipped in the juice of some dark-blue berries, he managed to scratch down a line or two to mark the days. His "huckleberry ink," I remember he called it.

And so it went, for I am not quite sure how long. Then, the Captain reported that he saw smoke on the distant island. All the others peered through his glass and confirmed him. Smoke there certainly was. That was all for several more days, and then one morning I remember the Captain and Jeremy Folger came racing up from shore to say that something was heading our way. What it was they could not yet make out, but they thought it looked like a number of low-lying open boats such as natives use. At all events, there was life on the water at last and it was coming toward us from the farther island. So the Captain called us all together to discuss what we should do in case they landed. Phoebe was playing in the door of the hut. She had made a house for me out of a beautifully colored conch shell Bill Buckle had found and fixed for me. We both listened to the talk that went on above us, so I remember it all perfectly.

The men were very grave under their beards and coats of tan. I knew that things were going to happen. It seemed like the moments before a thunderstorm.

"Think the chances are they'll be friendly, Bill?" the Captain was asking. "You've had more experience with natives than any of the rest of us."

Bill looked serious and stared off to sea thoughtfully.

"Well," he said finally, "these savages are one thing when they come alongside your vessel an' try to trade you coconuts for knives an' beads and calico, but they're another when they outnumber you ten to one an' you haven't got any gimcracks to humor 'em with, so I'm not for takin' chances 'way off here where they might be cannibals like as not!"

I saw the Captain frown and look uneasily toward his wife, who had turned pale at these last words.

"Not that I'm 'lottin' on any of us gettin' eaten up, ma'am," Bill hastened to reassure her, "only I say it's well to be prepared for anything."

All agreed to this and soon they were making plans. Jeremy and Reuben were to go down to the shore and hide our boats in a small cave they had discovered, while the Captain and Bill Buckle would remain to keep guard over us. Andy was all for going down to the shore, but Captain Preble ordered him to stay where he was. He also laid down the law to Phoebe.

"You're to do whatever I tell you," he told her, "no matter what 'tis. D'you understand?"

"Yes, Father," she answered. "Will they be all painted up like the Injuns at the Portland Fair?"

They all laughed a little at that, even Mrs. Preble. Then she made Phoebe bring me inside the hut with her. Andy had to come, too, but he insisted on staying in the opening that was our door to report what went on. The Captain and Bill Buckle took their places not far distant, each armed with a marlinspike he had brought from the boat. The Captain mourned the fact that his pistol was useless, for his small supply of ammunition had been ruined by salt water.

Andy had very sharp eyes and after some time he could make out that there were a great many boats, all keeping close together as they approached.

"Looks like there was 'most fifty of 'em all told," he reported, "but it's hard to tell with the sun shinin' down so bright. They're headin' this way sure enough."

It was the truth. By the time Reuben and Jeremy were back from their expedition, a host of brown men with no clothes to speak of were swarming up from shore. Some carried what looked like crude spears, others had rough shields, and still others spiked clubs. No one will ever be able to tell if they knew of our presence before they landed. As the Captain had pointed out, they might have seen smoke from the several fires we had made. Or, again, they might have come upon some hunting or fishing expedition. As I say, we never knew. Andy crouched in the door and told us all that he could make out.

"They've got up to the big tree now," he said. "The Cap'n an' Bill have stepped out an' kind of bowed to 'em. Now they've stopped. They're makin' signs together. I wonder if Bill knows what they mean?"

After a while he reported that they were all coming this way. It might have taken them five minutes to reach us, but I know it seemed like hours as we waited there together in the hut. I felt glad when I heard their footsteps padding close at hand. Captain Preble now peered in at the door, beckoning to us to come and stand beside him. I saw Mrs. Preble give one hand to Andy and take Phoebe's in her other and follow him out into the sunshine. It may have been the strong light after the half darkness of the hut, but at any rate there seemed to be hundreds of brown people swarming about us.

"Don't get wadgetty," I heard the Captain saying in a low voice. "They ain't done nothin' but look at us so far."

Look they certainly did. I have never seen so many bright, black eyes in so many peering faces. I caught sight of nose-rings and earrings under matted hair, of carved necklaces and bands of metal on wrists, arms, and ankles. It was the resourceful Bill Buckle who conceived the idea of taking off his shirt and exhibiting his tattoo marks. This caused a mur-mur of what we took to be interest to go about from mouth to mouth. They crowded round him till I thought he would be crushed by all the pressing brown bodies. Their curiosity lasted for some time and gave the rest of us a chance to talk a little among ourselves.

"They act like a parcel of children," Captain Preble said, "and I hope to glory they stay so."

Like children they easily tired of what had caught their attention, so next it was Phoebe about whom they began to crowd. This happened during a moment when she had let go her mother's hand. She had kept me pressed close to her during all this, and the biggest native with the most rings and beads on now caught sight of me between her fingers. He made a queer grunting noise at the rest and they all crowded about, pointing and gesticulating. I could feel Phoebe's heart thumping under me, but she did not flinch, not even when the big man, who must have been their Chief, since all the rest followed his slightest gesture, reached out and touched me with one enormous brown finger. He turned to the others with another grunt. Then he came back and held out his hand to her.

It was plain enough what he wanted. I knew, even before I heard the Captain's voice saying in that tone none dared disobey:

"Give her to him, Phoebe."

Years ago though it is, I cannot even think of that moment without a sense of creeping horror in every peg.

"Not Hitty, Father—" I heard Phoebe falter.

"You give her to him an' you do it quick." Only on that day of the fire on the *Diana-Kate* had I ever before heard the Captain speak so.

An ugly expression had crept over the big savage's face as Phoebe hesitated. He was speaking again to the rest and a murmur went round. Not a pleasant one to hear, I can tell you.

Phoebe did as she was told. The next thing I knew I was in his hands. It seemed hard to me to think that I had escaped from a crows' nest, from fire and the watery deep, only to fall at last into the hands of savages. But there being nothing I could do about it, I waited with what courage I could summon for him to make an end of me. Only a wrench or two with his fingers and I should be reduced to splinters of wood and a few cotton rags. I thought how terrible for Phoebe to see me broken to bits before her eyes. I think for the moment that all of us must have forgotten that I was made of the stuff which has power over evil.

All I can say is that it had power over that brown chief, for instead of finishing me off then and there, he continued to regard me with a sort of childlike awe. He turned me this way and that between his fingers; he moved my legs and arms with serious intentness and I must confess with as great consideration as I have ever known.

Then he beckoned the rest to his side and exhibited my feats for their benefit. Terrified as I was, I could not but take some pride in their open admiration.

"That doll's brought us luck and no mistake," I heard Bill Buckle saying to the Captain. "She knows how to handle 'em better 'n we do. They think she's some kind of a god, that's what, an' they ain't ever seen a jointed one."

"I believe you're right, Bill," the Captain agreed. "Look at how they watch her, real reverent and like they was in Meetin'."

"Well, I never did in all my born days!" exclaimed his wife. "I declare, Phoebe, I 'most believe what the peddler told you myself."

"Isn't he going to give her back to me?" Phoebe asked, stretching out her hand pleadingly toward me.

I saw Bill Buckle catch it quickly in his and pull her toward him.

"Steady there," he cautioned, "don't you make no sign of wantin' her." Then turning to her father he added, "If my mem'ry don't fail me, these natives have got some idea 'bout how if they take your god away from you they've got you in their power."

"That's true," Jeremy joined in. "I've heard folks say so. They won't do no harm to *us* long's they've got *her.*"

Whether or not the gesture that Phoebe had made had anything to do with it, I shall never know. Her hands had looked as if they were raised in prayer when she reached them out to me. At any rate, the natives seemed even more impressed by me and began making further grunts and motions.

"Well, Hitty," thought I to myself as the Chief lifted me up for them all to see, "a lot of queer things have happened to you—in the State of Maine and out of it—but this is certainly the queerest!"

At another grunt from him all the natives bowed their heads before me and went through more strange gesturings—and so I was carried away to become a heathen idol.

## CHAPTER VII
# In Which I Learn the Ways of Gods, Natives, and Monkeys

I have often wondered if any other doll was ever called upon to play such a role as mine? Here I was suddenly chosen to be god to a tribe of savages and with no more idea of what was expected of me than they would have had of how to behave in the church on Meeting House Hill. But in all fairness I must admit that I have seldom been treated with more consideration. They made me a little temple of green leaves and bamboo shoots to which I was conducted with great ceremony. I was set upon a sort of altar, trimmed with pink hibiscus flowers. As soon as these drooped, fresh ones were brought, also small offerings in the way of fruits and shells. If the responsibility of saving the lives of Phoebe Preble and all the rest had not weighed so heavily upon me, I fear that all this attention might very easily have turned my head.

As it was, I let the natives do as they wished with me, trusting to Providence that I might survive this experience as I had the others so far. I cannot say I was altogether happy when the Chief, who seemed to have my welfare very much at heart, removed my garments, one after the other, until I sat shamelessly upon my altar clad only in my muslin chemise. The only reason this had been spared to me was because of the red cross-stitch letters of my name, which in spite of salt water and sun had miraculously managed to keep some of their color. These seemed to attract their attention. I suppose they considered them some magic sign or spell, that must not be broken. How I blessed the day that Mrs. Preble had suggested Phoebe's sewing them there!

I was also forced to undergo some rather trying attempts at decorating my complexion according to South Sea Island ideas of beauty. Bright juices were squeezed from various berries and smeared on my face and body, till I dared not think of the outlandish appearance I must be cutting. But this I endured, as I would have endured far more, for the sake of those whose safety depended upon me. I did not object so much to some leaves and flowers they added or to a lump of red coral they hung about my neck on a thread of grass. This I took to be some sacred talisman. I trusted that my being of mountain-ash wood might keep off any evil power it possessed. In fact, I found myself counting for a great many things on those good properties which the Old Peddler had said were in me. Those were days in which I had need of all the power I could summon.

It is rather lonely to be a god for days on end. Perhaps I should have felt differently about this if I had been able to understand what the brown men said to one another when they made their queer gruntings before my temple. But they never knew if I felt bored or frightened. I continued to smile down upon them as serenely as if I had been back on a State of Maine mantelpiece. I had been made with a pleasant expression, so it was really no credit to me. I longed above all else to know what had become of Phoebe and the others, but only once or twice did I catch the sound of familiar voices among the trees not far away, and once I thought I recognized Bill Buckle and Jeremy in the distance. How many days and nights passed thus I do not know, for I soon lost count of them in my new position.

But it was during this time that I came to know monkeys and their ways as I never should have come to know them otherwise. At first, it made me very uneasy to have them clambering about in the branches all round me, with their crazy chatterings and their lean and supple tails. They had a way of coming close and staring me almost out of countenance, and some of the bolder ones even poked me with their skinny paws. Their fingers were thin and inquisitive and they used them for all the world like human beings. This made me both uncomfortable and envious. I did not think it fair for these wild creatures to have ten whole fingers, while I must get along as best I could with my two clumsy wooden mittens. However, as I became more lonely and the monkeys grew more used to me, we struck up a sort of friendship. The kindliness and delicacy of their hands reassured me in time and I came to enjoy the touch of their fingers when they stroked me curiously, as they sometimes did. There was one smallish monkey with a silvery-white face and an especially active tail, who paid me considerable attention. I almost came to understand his chatterings, and his visits helped to break the monotony of my days and nights. Once I remember he even brought me a present. I think it must have been a nutmeg, at any rate it looked like those I have met with since on pantry shelves. I think he expected me to eat it, but though I was unable to show him my thanks in this way, I let it lie in my lap till one of his more mischievous mates made off with it.

Bright tropic birds flew and sang about me, shining green lizards sometimes slid about my temple floor, and so I continued this life until the night of my rescue. Of this I had had no warning whatever. Indeed, I had been able to learn nothing of the fate of my family, nor had I caught even a glimpse of them of late. I had no idea whether they knew where the natives had hidden me. I only hoped they did.

Then one night, as my captors slept in a circle not far from my temple, I heard the unmistakable sound of stealthy human footsteps coming nearer and nearer. There was no moon, scarcely any light except from a star or two that showed through the branches of the palm trees. I had no idea whether it was friend or foe, but something told me that I should know before many more minutes passed.

After a while I felt a stirring in the branches below me. My temple was set rather high upon woven shoots and these now began to shake perilously. I felt fearful that the savages might hear and become roused. I had no wish to be in the midst of a skirmish, for those natives' clubs would make short work of me.

Someone was drawing short, panting breaths quite close to me now. I felt them warm on my face. Then a hand closed round me. I felt myself being lifted off my perch and borne away still in the hot, clutching hand.

As we sped through the hot, soft darkness, something about that hand seemed to reassure me. I knew I had felt its touch before, and even in the midst of such danger, I felt more secure than I had in many days and nights. Now we had cleared the thicker palm trees and I was able to make out the features of my rescuer—dim, but unmistakably Andy.

He sped toward the shore, moving stealthily in his bare feet and looking over his shoulder every once in so often to make sure no one was following us.

"Fooled 'em that time," I heard him mutter with satisfaction as he ran.

Suddenly, out of nowhere, as it seemed, arose the form of Jeremy Folger. I could have wept for joy at the sight of his crooked back.

"What you doin' here?" he asked in a whisper. "I thought you was along of the rest."

"I went back a ways after somethin'." Andy spoke evasively and kept me behind him. "Ain't the boats ready yet?"

"'Most," Jeremy told him. "One's sprung a bad leak though. Looks like we'll all have to crowd in one, an' that's not so good when it comes to makin' time."

From more of their whispered words I gathered that a vessel was in sight. At least it had been that afternoon. Captain Preble had dared not make any attempt at signaling or putting off in the boats for fear of rousing the natives, who had not been acting in any too friendly a way of late. However, it was now or never, they all agreed. It was a desperate chance, for should they not be able to reach the ship in time to signal for help, the natives would no doubt be hostile if they returned. It had been necessary to wait for darkness to get the boats out of hiding. Even now there was no knowing when some savage might surprise them at their preparations and alarm the rest.

Now we were on shore, in a small, sheltered cove, well hidden from view. I could just make out the dark shapes of Captain Preble and the rest. Phoebe and her mother were already in the stern seat of one boat and the men were standing up to their thighs in the water, loading in the few belongings still left us. This must be managed with great care to keep the boat trimmed well. The Captain spoke tensely. I knew from the tones of his voice that he was more worried than he would have admitted. When he caught sight of Andy he began giving him a piece of his mind for having left them.

"You're a fine sailor," he scolded, "runnin' off at a time like this. If I wasn't so pressed I declare I'd give you a whippin' you wouldn't soon forget. 'T would serve you right to get left behind to spend your days with the savages."

Andy took this scolding in good part. But when the Captain was through he drew me out from behind his back.

"I went after Hitty," he explained, holding me out. At this Phoebe started up in the boat, so that it rocked perilously.

"Sit down, Phoebe!" commanded her father. "Yes, it's Hitty, right enough."

He took me from Andy and turned me about in his hands a moment before he passed me on to Phoebe.

"So that's what you were up to?" he asked Andy in quite a different tone. "Didn't you know you might have got yourself killed for touchin' her?"

"Yes, sir," said Andy rather sheepishly, "but I found out where they was keepin' her an' when Phoebe cried 'bout havin' to go off an' leave her behind, I thought I'd try to fetch her along."

"It's a wonder we ain't all dead now," put in Bill Buckle.

"'T won't be no afternoon tea party if they find she's gone and put out after us!" warned Reuben.

"Yes," I heard Jeremy agree, "our lives won't be worth much 'round here once they find out, but I swear I'm glad he done it. That doll deserves a chance to get saved as much as the rest of us."

"You're right," Captain Preble said. "Get in and pull for all you're worth, boys, and Andy, you set's far up the bow's you can and watch out sharp for lights ahead. That vessel wasn't makin' much headway this afternoon. I hope to heaven she ain't been beatin' it up any since."

Phoebe had me in her hands again as we slid out into the waters of the little cove.

"Oh, Mother," she sighed, "I'll never be cross to Andy again as long as I live, and when we get home I'm going to give him my silver mug and porringer to keep forever and ever."

"Mercy, child," her mother sighed, "how can you talk of things like that when we don't even know if we stand a chance o' sightin' that ship, an' if we don't—"

She did not finish her sentence, but I knew what was in her mind. It was perhaps the most dangerous of all the situations we had been in, for if that vessel had got out of our reach we should be in a pretty pickle indeed. Once the natives found me gone, it would be certain death to return to the island. In that case there would be nothing left to do but float at sea till our supply of food and water gave out or we all went to the bottom. I knew all this and yet, despite everything, I would not have exchanged my place in Phoebe Preble's lap for the most beautiful temple of ivory and sandalwood ever fashioned by the most admiring tribe of savages. But I suppose that is the nature of dolls. I am sure anyone would have felt as I did during that long, eventful night.

It was very crowded and uncomfortable with all of us in the boat, and it sat so low in the water that a particularly big wave often drenched us. I did not mind this so much as the others, however, for I hoped these wettings would remove some of my outlandish berry-juice decorations before it was light enough for Phoebe to see them. There was very little wind, and while this made it useless to hoist our small canvas sail, still it meant that the other ship would have to tack and veer to make any headway. If conditions continued like this and the men could keep steadily at their oars, the Captain thought our chances of hailing the ship were about even. They worked in shifts—first the Captain and Jeremy would pull at the oars and the others steer and keep a lookout, then they would change about and Bill Buckle and Reuben would row while the others watched and kept us on our course by means of the small compass. Captain Preble had his lantern in readiness. Fortunately, he had kept it safely with a small supply of oil, which he had hoarded against just this need. He had his flint and steel in his pocket and the moment the ship's light was sighted he intended to begin signaling.

The stars that hung low on the horizon often confused even such seasoned old sailors as Bill and Jeremy into believing they saw the longed-for light. After each such mistake, the spirits of all in the boat-load would drop, though the men never slackened at their posts. The warm tropic water was alive with the most brilliant phosphorescence I have ever seen. Each time our oars dipped and rose again they made showers of shining miniature stars on either side. Phoebe said they were fishes' eyes looking up at us from the dark water. But her mother did not think much of the sight. She said it made her dizzy to look, and there was only one light that would do us any good. And still the men pulled on and still there was no sign of it.

Worn out, Phoebe fell asleep at last, against her mother. I

continued to stay bolt upright in her lap, for I could not but feel still that much depended upon me, though in this case I must admit that all the credit went to the men as they bent and pulled with aching arms and backs.

"We'd ought to sight her any minute now," the Captain kept telling them. But as the minutes turned into hours and still no masthead lantern loomed ahead, they grew more and more silent, pulling doggedly and wasting no breath on words or questions.

Andy lay huddled in the bow. I supposed he, too, had fallen asleep, when suddenly he gave a cry.

"There 't is," he shouted, "on our port side, plain's anything!"

"He's right," Jeremy affirmed. "I can just make her out."

Instantly the men were all alertness again. They gave a shout or two to express their feelings and then bent to their oars with renewed vigor. Mrs. Preble trembled and Phoebe woke and hugged me close for joy.

"She's still a good ways off," Captain Preble said, squinting through his glass. "Give me that oar, Reuben, while I lash the lantern to it."

After this had been done, he began trying to light the wick. This took some time and he cursed and muttered under his breath as he struggled. Finally he had it lighted, but it flickered feebly.

"That'll never do us no good," he decided as he watched it. "Wick must've been poor to begin with and I guess salt water ain't improved it any. Whose shirt'll we burn first?"

By this time there was very little clothing left to any of the party. Reuben had gone stripped to his waist ever since we had left the *Diana-Kate*, Bill Buckle's shirt had fallen away to nothing on the Island, and Jeremy's was little more than a tattered lace-work on his back. However, he peeled this off and handed it over without a word. Captain Preble poured on it a little of the precious oil from the lantern and soon it was blazing on top of the hoisted oar. When it was almost gone, the Captain's went the same way. After that, his wife removed her petticoat. That burned for a long time and made a fine blaze once it got going. In the queer, high light from these makeshift torches I could see the men's faces, streaked with sweat, as they pulled toward our goal. They were very tired now. Each stroke was slower and more of an effort than the last, in spite of all they could do. And still that light showed only like a far star beyond our port bow.

"Seems like we'll never get there at this rate," Andy said at last. "Ain't they ever goin' to sight us?"

It was the same thought in all their minds, but none dared venture more lest they lose what little strength they had left.

It even seemed to me that the light looked farther away than it had an hour or so before, and I knew that if this were true and they did not sight our flares before daylight, we were indeed in a sorry plight. I think I must almost have read the thoughts going on in the Captain's mind, for presently he said:

"Oil's 'most gone now, so bring out what you've got and we'll make one more try."

I wondered what more the men could give, since by this time they were nearly as bare as the natives. Mrs. Preble must have wondered, too, for I heard her speaking above me.

"Here, Dan'l," she said, "take my bonnet 'n' shawl. And here's my other petticoat, too. This ain't any time to worry over appearances."

The Captain collected these and Phoebe's little muslin waist. I saw Mrs. Preble give a last regretful look at the shawl as it lay between her feet. It was her best and she had tied her belongings in it when we left the *Diana-Kate*. Somehow it seemed like our last link with the old days. She watched it soaked in the oil and set alight without a murmur and none of us saw anything funny in the sight of her beaver bonnet blazing away along with it on top of the oar. They made a great light as the Captain and Reuben held it hoisted as high as their arms could reach.

"If that don't fetch 'em, we might's well throw the oars overboard an' ourselves after 'em," I heard Bill Buckle say to Jeremy in a low tone. I would gladly have offered my chemise too, but common sense told me that it would make no more light than a firefly.

Now the torch was burning out. When the last flame wavered and failed, I saw Captain Preble drop the little knot of shriveled, black cloth into the water. No one moved or lifted a hand to the rowing. We all realized there would be no use in that. Every eye was fixed on that far speck of light that meant so much to seven souls and a wooden doll.

Suddenly I saw the Captain's hands go out in a quick gesture. Another light had appeared beside the other. Now another and another shot up.

"They've sighted us, praise be!" he cried. "They're sendin' up flares to tell us they're comin'."

He was trembling so he could hardly reach for the oar. Reuben had slumped down in his seat with his face between his hands, and Bill Buckle and Jeremy were sobbing like Mrs. Preble and Phoebe. I would have cried, too, if I had been able.

## CHAPTER VIII

# In Which I Am Lost in India

We were taken aboard the *Hesper* about daybreak and before long we felt almost as much at home there as on the *Diana-Kate*. She was a trim, well-built vessel engaged in the India and China trade, though lately crippled in a severe storm. This accident had sent her miles out of her proper course and the captain and crew had been forced to put in at a remote harbor to repair damages. So when we sighted her she was proceeding on her way with a makeshift keel.

Her captain hailed from our part of the world, from Fairhaven, in Massachusetts, if I remember right, where he had left a wife and children. A more kindly or courteous man never sailed the seas. I shall always hold him in grateful remembrance because of the gallant way in which he offered his best silk handkerchief to wrap me when Phoebe showed him the sorry state of my wardrobe. It was a voluminous handkerchief of rich crimson silk with anchors and twisted ropes woven all round the border. I had need of every inch of it, too, considering that the natives had left me only my chemise. The rest of our party were less well fitted out than I. The men accepted any shirt or trousers that could be spared regardless of size or fit, and Mrs. Preble concocted two queer-looking garments for herself and Phoebe from a length of calico. This had been brought along for possible trading with natives and was therefore gaudy beyond all description.

"I'd be run right out of Meetin' at home if they ever found out I'd put such colors on my back," she said when it was brought out.

Still, it was cloth, and she managed to cut and sew it with the coarse sail needles and thread the men furnished. There was not any too much material and Phoebe's dress resembled a walking piece-bag when she had it on. Captain Preble promised, however, that we should all be fitted out at our next port of call. He still had the little bag of gold which he had worn about his neck ever since we had left the *Diana-Kate*. It was the only ready money he would see for many a long day, he said, but he was not one to hoard it at such a time.

He and his three mates used to sit by the hour dolefully figuring up what our losses in sperm oil must amount to.

"Still, it's a mercy we're alive to tell the tale," someone would always remind the others sooner or later.

It was much cleaner being aboard a trader than it had been in our whaling days. Considering that we had lost all but our lives, it was amazing how well our little party kept up its spirits. The crew were a friendly lot and Phoebe and I were soon on excellent terms with them all. She liked nothing better than to recount my exploits to an admiring group of sailors, and though she had removed all traces of my berry-juice stains, she would point out just where these had been. The men appeared quite impressed.

"'T ain't every doll has had her advantages," they agreed. "You don't think maybe she'll miss bein' an idol once you get her back home?"

They need have had no fears on that ground.

Our next port would be Bombay and we soon began making many plans about what we should buy there. The *Hesper's* captain had promised to bring his little girl a string of coral beads, and he said that Phoebe should have one, too. Andy wanted a knife with an ivory handle and Captain Preble said his wife should have the handsomest shawl they could find to make up for the one that had been burned in the long-boat. There had been so many delays and accidents all round that no boat-load of people was ever more anxious to make port. Never, I am sure, has a more joyful cry gone up at sight of land than the men's when at last the long-looked-for coast line appeared.

"Now," said our new captain, as we came to anchor, "we'll take the day off and all go ashore to see the folks and fashions."

Such a host of little things come back to me as I think of that day—the queer boats, the domes and narrow streets, the whining beggars, and the throngs of robed and turbaned men who walked with a smooth sureness of foot I have never seen in any other place. Sometimes we passed half-naked men with their legs or arms tied up in knots or with their bodies twisted in a manner both grotesque and horrible.

"Fakirs, they call 'em," the captain of the *Hesper* told us.

"Horrible," gasped Mrs. Preble, as we passed close to one old man who had let his arms grow together in a way that made one shiver. "It's plain indecent, that's what it is. Come right along, Phoebe, and don't look at such sights."

One of the crew knew his way about the city well and could even speak enough of the native tongue to get us about and our purchases made. After all those months at sea it was no wonder such an expedition went to all their heads. I began to grow worried, fearing that there could not possibly be money enough to pay for all they were buying. By noon we had collected embroidered India muslins for best, more durable cotton prints, and the most marvelously patterned cashmere shawl to take the place of the old one. Besides, there were all sorts of trinkets, for whatever caught Phoebe Preble's fancy sooner or later managed to find its way into her hands or her father's pockets. She soon had strings of silver and coral and little twinkling shells. There was even a string for me, of round red coral. Our guide swore it had been intended to be worn as a nose ring, but it was a perfect fit for my neck. They all declared it became me wonderfully, and Phoebe felt sure that when my new India muslin was made I would be quite a Queen of Sheba among dolls. Alas, how little did we guess that this was to be our last day together!

And so the hours passed as one strange sight after another beckoned us. I shall never hear distant bells ringing without remembering the sound of some far ones I heard that day. I suppose they came from an Indian temple. We saw elephants and tigers and sacred white bullocks being led in a procession through the streets. We bargained and gaped in dim bazaars, and the rest of the party ate rice and curry and sweetmeats in a place the sailor knew where men made weird music all the time with little drums and reed flutes. Indeed, we saw and did so much that by mid-afternoon Phoebe Preble began to lag behind the rest and complain of being tired. Since there were still many things to be bought and the two captains had much other business to attend to, it was decided that Bill Buckle should take Phoebe back to the *Hesper*.

We were still a long distance from the harbor, and the child was so tired that Bill took pity on her and decided to give us a ride back. He took her up in his arms and soon we were jogging comfortably, well above the crowds of brown people. This afforded me a fine view. I could see over Bill's shoulder and miss nothing of all that was passing. Not usually being in a position so fortunate, I made the most of it. I felt very well content, as is so often the case when we have the least reason to be.

I shall never be sure how it happened. But I think the steady motion of Bill's long strides, added to the long, hot day of excitement, must have proved too much for Phoebe. Her head dropped lower and lower till it rested on Bill's shoulder and she was as fast asleep as if she had been at home in bed. Bill Buckle strode on, carrying her as easily as if she had been a bundle from one of the bazaars. As for me, I dangled now from Phoebe's hand, which hung over his shoulder. It was a rather precarious position and I knew it; still, I did not realize my actual danger till I felt myself slipping from her hold.

I made one vain effort to steer myself against Bill Buckle and so attract his attention. But I could do nothing to help myself. I fell free of them both, flat on my face in an unknown gutter.

The stones were so hard and the fall so unexpected that I lay there in a daze for I know not how long. My wooden frame shivered from the impact and the thick foreign mud rendered me almost senseless. Still, I was well aware of the disaster that had overtaken me, especially when I recalled Phoebe's sleepiness and knew that it might be the better part of an hour before she awoke and missed me. Innumerable brown feet passed close by, some even over me, but as most of them were swift and bare and I lay in a hollow with so much mud, I was not seriously hurt. However, when I thought of the elephants I had seen passing earlier in the day and remembered the size and clumsiness of their feet, I felt in no way reassured. The babble of strange voices uttering heathenish gibberish above me only added to my misery and despair, though I strained with all my might to catch the sound of a familiar voice and words that I could understand.

"Lost in India," I thought to myself, "I, who have so miraculously survived the elements, not to mention those Island savages, to perish like this in a foreign land!"

I could feel my new coral beads about my neck. They were round and smooth and I knew how fine a color they had been when Phoebe chose them for me from among the others in the bazaar. We had both felt so proud then. Now they were as ashes and brimstone to me. How gladly would I have exchanged them for the welcome pressure of Phoebe's thumb and forefinger! Common sense told me that even should my absence be discovered soon, and a search started, it would be well-nigh impossible to find me where I lay. Still, I continued to hope on, as who would not in such a predicament?

No, I never saw Phoebe or any of the Preble family again, though once I did hear news of them in a roundabout fashion. But that belongs to a later chapter. She must be dead a good many years now, even if she lived to be a very old lady, for that was over a hundred years ago and she was not made of mountain-ash wood. How strange it all seems, and yet the cross-stitch letters of my name that she worked so carefully into my chemise are still plain. I hear people remark upon them as they look me over in the Antique Shop.

But to return to Bombay and the gutter. My next recollection is of being lifted up by long and supple brown fingers. These belonged to a little brown old man in a turban and rather ragged, flowing robes. The captain's red silk handkerchief, in which I had been wrapped when Phoebe dropped me, had evidently attracted the attention of his wonderfully keen, black eyes. At any rate, he picked me up, turned me this way and that, seemed about to toss me away again, then changed his mind, and finally, wiping me off on a corner of his voluminous robe, bore me away with him, I knew not where.

The next thing I knew I was upon the hard stone floor of a small room. It was dark now and only a little moonlight came in through a high, grated window. I was lying close to a large wicker basket from which issued the most extraordinary rustlings. They were like no others I have ever heard. I cannot describe them more than to say that they filled me with foreboding. I felt sure that no good whatsoever could come out of that basket. Indeed, I would have given my coral beads gladly to be well out of its way instead of so near it.

Presently, in the dim light I saw the turbaned Hindoo who had taken me out of the gutter appear with another turbaned figure. Together they crouched on the floor nearby and from under his robes the Hindoo produced a native flute or flageolet. It was made of bamboo, I think, and gave out a thin, reedy sound, almost as weird as the rustlings. I cannot describe the feelings that this music gave me. It seemed to produce strange sensations in all my pegs. I had had no idea that I could be so completely sad just from listening to certain sounds made over and over by blowing into a bit of hollow wood.

And then the basket became alive with further unaccountable

rustlings. I saw the cover quiver and rise a little. Meantime, the sad, sad music continued. I was unhappy enough in my present situation without this. Still, I could not but continue to stare at the basket lid in horrified fascination as it was slowly raised inch by inch from within. At last it was shoved more forcibly back and I saw the head and lithe body of a great hooded cobra. Jeremy had pointed one out to Andy earlier in the day, but that had been safely behind the bars of a cage. There was nothing but the queer music to restrain this one. Horrified and yet at the same time fascinated, I watched it uncoil itself, slip out of the basket, and begin to creep toward the Hindoo. Now he stopped his music an instant and the snake also stopped, even in the midst of a glide. Now he would begin to play more quickly and it would increase its pace. It was as if the music willed it to do this or that and the slippery, coiling creature could not but follow its commands. As it swayed, it would move its head with its layers of skin, fold on fold, slowly from side to side. I saw the glitter of bright, lidless eyes and the flicker of a darting tongue; I heard its scales making a faint scraping sound on the floor. Once, even, it came very close to me, so close that I felt part of its chilly body slide across my feet. At the touch I stiffened till it seemed I must surely crack in two, and had it not been that my hair was so firmly painted on my head I have no doubt but that it would have stood on end.

Still, as I have said, one can become accustomed to anything in due course of time—even to great hooded cobras. I was never to be exactly upon friendly terms with this creature, but after several days I came to take him more calmly. I learned that the Hindoo held him completely in his

Had my hair not been so firmly painted on my head, it
would have stood on end.

power and that, after all, he was a rather patient and long-suffering snake, going through his paces as many times a day as his master directed by means of the flageolet.

Stouter dolls than I might have quailed at being pressed into service by a Hindoo snake-charmer. I cannot say it is a stage of my career that I enjoy remembering, but at least I comfort myself with the thought that I did not behave in any way which would bring disgrace upon my kind.

My rôle was a passive one—to stand by like a sort of image while the Hindoo and his snake went through their strange capers. I even traveled about in the snake basket, though, let me hasten to add, in the compartment which contained the food and cooking things, not the cobra.

Being a snake-charmer in India in those days was apparently not a way to make much money. I am sure the Hindoo would not have taken me on as a performer in his troupe if I had needed any food. He himself ate mostly boiled rice, and when we were in country places, the cobra managed to take care of his appetite with lizards, flies and the like. Perhaps this was one reason why we traveled about so much, but I suspect it is the way with all snake-charmers to be on the move. At any rate, we must have gone nearly the length and breadth of India, or so it seemed to me, before I heard a familiar word or saw a white face.

Once more, time meant little to me and it may have been years or again only a few weeks that I journeyed in the wicker basket. At any rate, I had grown quite discouraged over the state of my affairs. I had abandoned all hope of rescue and felt that I should end my days in heat and dust, far, far from my native State of Maine. Which only goes to show how little any of us can tell about our own futures.

At last one afternoon toward sunset, when the day had been a shade more hot and dusty than usual, we stopped by a long, low building that somehow wore a different look from the rest in the town. Quite a group of native children and others gathered about the Hindoo. Soon he had his flageolet at his lips and the snake was being put through its paces. As usual, I had been set out beside the basket, still wrapped in the rather dingy and tattered red handkerchief and my chemise and coral beads. And then, quite without warning, just as the cobra was sliding toward its master before the eyes of the straggling crowd, I heard a voice saying words that I could understand.

They were very simple words, but I can never say what a combination of homesickness and relief they brought to me there in that place.

"Hurry, my dear," was what I heard, "we shall be late getting home."

At that moment I saw a man and a woman draw near. They were brown, but no darker than the Prebles had been on the Island, and their clothes, though very plain and rather faded, were like those at home. For a moment I feared they would pass by. Something must have attracted the woman's attention, for she motioned to the man to stop. They stood together, a little on the edge of the crowd, watching the snake and his master perform their queer antics. Suddenly I saw the woman touch the man on the arm and point toward me.

I realized that they had noticed me, and there I was, unable to move so much as a single peg, to express my joy, or to beg them to rescue me from my plight. But once again Providence or the power of mountain-ash wood intervened. I heard the lady saying: "I am sure it is not an Indian doll, William. Look at the expression and her hair. She couldn't have been made anywhere but at home."

"I declare she does have a familiar look," he agreed. "What would you think of getting her for Thankful?"

"I was just thinking of her," said the lady. "Here she is growing up so far from home and not even a doll to play with. I suppose," she added, "it is rather dirty."

"Well, we ought to be able to remedy that," he answered with a smile. "Think of all the souls we came here to wash clean of their sins."

I thought the lady seemed more interested in my appearance than in what he meant and I must say it seemed a far more important matter to me then. To this day I shall always believe they did as much good by restoring me to my proper place as a doll as they did by all their baptizing and hymn-singing. The man could speak the Hindoo's language, and soon he was bargaining for me. It took some time, and I had fears that the Hindoo would not accept the sum offered. Finally he did, and I was handed over to the lady, who kept me wrapped in her handkerchief as if I had been a leper.

Still, I was in no mood to criticize. I submitted with good grace to a scrubbing with soap and water as thorough as I have ever endured. During my overhauling, I listened to various scraps of conversation and learned that I had fallen into the hands of some missionaries, who had come out to this remote station in the hills. Here they had established a church and school and here they helped nurse and convert as many natives as possible. Their only child, Little Thankful, had been born here and it was for her that I had been bought.

"It's just as I said," I heard her mother tell her father after my scrubbing. "It makes me homesick just to look at her honest American face."

"Yes," said he, "now you've got her clean, she resembles my sister Ruth back in Delaware."

"I mean to dress her just the way I used to when I was a little girl," his wife went on, "so Thankful will get used to something besides robes and turbans before she goes back. This must have belonged to some other child, for see, William, here's her name worked in cross-stitch on her little chemise. It's real fine linen and I mean to wash it out myself. She must have been with nice people, poor thing. I wonder how that dirty old snake-charmer ever got his hands on her."

"God moves in a mysterious way," he responded. "I must confess that it has touched me strangely to have this little doll cast upon our very doorstep just in time to answer our own child's needs. If it would not seem like too great a liberty to take, I could find it in my heart to preach a sermon about our finding her when we gather for prayers tonight."

"I think I should wait, William, if I were you," his wife cautioned. "I should not want Little Thankful to find out about her till we have her dressed and ready for the child's birthday next week. High time she had a doll to tend."

So I was to appear at a birthday celebration in the near future and belong to a little girl again! I could think of nothing else that night as I lay tucked carefully out of sight in a sewing-box where Little Thankful could not find me.

## CHAPTER IX
# In Which I Have Another Child
# to Play with Me

If I devote less space to my days with Little Thankful, it is not that I was unhappy during the two years I was her doll but simply that other periods of my life have been more eventful. I was presented to her on the morning of her fourth birthday and I saw her well started into her sixth year. I cannot truthfully say that she lived up to her name, but I doubt if many children could do so, and though she had been born in a missionary station and reared to the sound of hymn-tunes and sermons from babyhood, she possessed as high spirits as any child I ever belonged to. In fact, her temper was not always dependable. But doubtless this was because she had no children of her own kind to play with, and the native nurse who tended her gave in to her whims at every turn. It was indeed high time she had a doll, and though she never lavished the same amount of care and affection upon me as Phoebe Preble had, still, I must in all justice say that she never treated me unkindly until—but I have not reached the place for that yet.

Little Thankful's mother was better at hymns and Bible lessons than dressing dolls. However, I was so glad to feel decent cloth upon my back again that I was in no mood to insist upon the latest fashions. She made me a rather voluminous dress of cotton print, in a far from gaudy pattern. It nearly covered my painted feet, and the ruffle about my neck practically hid my coral beads. But these were small matters. I was clean and comfortable and I belonged to a little girl again.

If life seemed quiet and somewhat dull at times in that remote station in the hills, with nothing more exciting than an occasional package of letters from the outside world or a baptizing of newly converted natives, at least I knew that I was safe and in good hands. During this time I had leisure and a chance to improve my mind more than heretofore. All through the long, burning midday heat, as we sat in the dimness within doors, while native boys ran barefoot about their household tasks or pulled at the fan ropes to make a breath of air in the room, Little Thankful's mother taught her to read and write a little and add up to fifty. She also taught her Bible texts, the catechism, and many hymns.

I must confess that this made me a little uneasy at first. There was a part about remembering "our frame, that we are dust," which rather alarmed me until I remembered that this did not apply to me, since I was not made of dust at all but of good solid ash wood. After that I did not let any of the phrases, no matter how strange they sounded, bother me. The hymns were more to my taste and I committed a number of them to memory as Little Thankful droned them out after her mother. Some impressed me so greatly that I can even say parts of them to this day. I remember one favorite that began:

> *From Greenland's icy mountains,*
> *From India's coral strand,*
> *Where Afric's sunny fountains*

*Roll down their golden sand. . . .*

This seemed particularly appropriate to me; also, the verse:

*In vain with lavish kindness*
*The gifts of God are strown,*
*The heathen in his blindness*
*Bows down to wood and stone.*

But I felt that this hymn could teach me little after all my experiences on the Island. I wondered what Little Thankful's parents would say if they knew that they were entertaining in their midst one who had been just such an idol?

Little Thankful was working on a sampler, too, with roses and doves and a weeping willow. It had a verse as well, which I can still recall:

*While Beauty and Pleasure and Passion hold sway*
*And Folly and Fashion would lure us away.*
*O, let not these Phantoms our wishes engage,*
*Let us live so in Youth that we blush not in age.*

I thought this rather disheartening advice, but Little Thankful took it to heart not at all.

Then one day when she was well past her fifth birthday and growing tall and active, Little Thankful fell ill of a serious fever. I do not know much about it except that she lay in a stupor for many days, and her father and mother used one after another of their best remedies, but all to no avail. Her nurse

Little Thankful's sampler had doves and a weeping willow
tree on it.

scarcely left the bedside, but finally, when the fever went from bad to worse, she slipped out and returned stealthily with a native doctor. For some time he studied the little girl in the big bed, felt her hands and forehead, and made some curious passes above her with his long brown hands. Then he went away, leaving with the old woman some herbs and directions for brewing them. She evidently knew that Little Thankful's parents would not approve of native treatment, for she had managed this all in secret, and how she was able to cook the herbs as he had told her, I shall never know. At all events, she was determined upon saving her charge's life. I myself saw her slip in and administer the dose while the child's mother was out of the sick-room for a moment.

Whether it was the native remedies or the doses from the family medicine chest or Little Thankful's own spirit I shall never know; perhaps it was all three of these things working together, but at last she was strong enough to get up and move about, although she was far from her old lively self. So her father and mother put their heads together and decided that it was high time she returned to America.

"This is no climate for children," they told each other one night after she was asleep. I could hear them from where I sat on a light-stand beside her bed. "We might as well make up our minds to send her back to Philadelphia, the first chance we get."

Philadelphia, I had heard, was where Little Thankful's grandparents lived, her mother's people. They had never seen their granddaughter and every letter from them begged to have her sent to live in the old house where her mother had been born and brought up before her.

"Yes," agreed her father and mother, "it is not good for the child to grow up in such a place as this. Much as we shall miss her, she must go."

Go we did. There had been much bustle and many preparations beforehand. Word had come unexpectedly of friends who would undertake the care of Little Thankful on the long voyage, and immediately our things were packed and we started on a long journey by bullock cart over rough mountain roads. At last, by devious ways and a flat river boat, we reached lower lands again. I had not known that the Hindoo snake-charmer had brought me such a long distance, though it had seemed far enough at the time. Once again I found myself in the thronging streets of Bombay; once again I was to be a passenger aboard a sailing vessel, and homeward bound.

There was a very sad leave-taking when Little Thankful said good-bye to her parents. They would not in all probability see her for five more years, so it was no wonder they cried as they watched her go away with the ladies from another mission station. These two were middle-aged and unused to children, as the child discovered before we had been settled twenty-four hours on the boat, a fine clipper called *The Rainbow*. Their idea of looking out for her was to hear her repeat her prayers night and morning, see that she ate porridge for breakfast, and occasionally administer a large dose of calomel. All very well as far as it went, but Little Thankful had plenty of chance to get into mischief at the same time. After the first few weeks out, her own parents would scarcely have known the child. She made almost as free of the ship as Phoebe Preble had done, though she was less clever and adventurous at climbing the ratlines. Her sandy hair, usually kept brushed as smooth as satin, now blew about her shoulders in wild disorder. Her face had almost as many freckles to the square inch as Andy had been able to boast on the Island, and the ruffles of her pantalettes and petticoats were in disgraceful tatters. If the good ladies attempted to do anything about this, Little Thankful would be away and out of their sight with the swiftness of a squirrel. So finally they gave up and let her go her own way.

She made many friends also among the crew, but the captain of this ship was not one to take up with children or passengers. Of these I saw little or nothing, for I spent more time in the stuffy cabin, which Little Thankful shared with one of the missionary ladies, than I had done on either of my previous voyages. However, I could see blue water and hear the familiar sounds of shouted orders, of wind in the rigging, and the chanteys the men sang as they hauled on their lines. Every day I knew brought me nearer to the shores which I continued to regard as home, though I had spent far more time away than upon them.

And so our voyage drew to a close, cleaner, of course, because of the lack of whale-oil, but also, by the same token, less eventful. We saw the shores of the Carolinas early one morning and after that it was only a matter of a few days and one or two stops at other ports for discharging cargo before we came to our destination.

My first recollection of Philadelphia is of driving through its pleasant brick-lined streets very early one morning as Little Thankful's grandfather took us to his house. It was a sunny April day, the hoofs of the fine pair of horses clattered briskly over the cobblestones, and by nearly every door a maid was out scouring the steps or polishing the brass door-knockers.

Trees in green bud showed in yards or little open squares and there was much bustle of tradesmen opening the shutters of their neat, well-kept shops. I wanted to cry out for joy at such sights and at the gilt weathervane topping the pointed steeple of a church we passed. I was upon familiar ground again, and I felt happier than I had done since I became parted from the Prebles.

Little Thankful and I were soon the center of attention in a brick house with white trimmings and three short steps that led straight from the front door to the pavement. It was on Christian Street, so it seemed no wonder to me that the daughter of the family should have turned into a missionary and gone off to save the heathen. The house inside was much more elaborate than the Prebles', though far less roomy and rambling. The fireplaces were smaller, the rooms narrow with quite elaborate glass lamps from which dangled crystal points. All the furniture looked very handsome and solemn and as if no child had used it for many years, as was, indeed, the case.

Little Thankful's grandmother was a plump old lady with the whitest hair and the pinkest cheeks and the most dimpled pair of hands I have ever seen. She dressed in rustling black silk and lace caps with long pleated streamers that stood out on either side when she bustled about. She bustled a great deal that first day, continually shaking her head or making little clicking noises with her teeth over the sorry state of her granddaughter's wardrobe.

"Dear, dear," she sighed to her husband, "it's just as I said— India's no place to bring up children. But it's worse than I expected. The poor child hasn't even a merino or a dimity to her name, and as for her bodices and her undermuslins, really it pains me to think that a grandchild of mine should come to such a pass."

"You must buy all the materials she needs tomorrow, my dear," the old man assured her, "the very best you can find, and get a seamstress in directly. I want her to be as well set up as any other little girl in Philadelphia. How'll that suit you, Miss Thankful, eh?"

But her grandmother could only shake her head some more.

"That's all very well," she said, "but it'll take weeks and I promised the Pryces she should go to their party tomorrow."

Little Thankful was all excited at the idea of this event, for it was to be her first party, as it was to be mine. Her grandmother took us out shopping in the morning, where I was dazed by all the fine stores. In those days, ready-made dresses had not been invented. It would have seemed a real calamity not to have one's clothes fitted and stitched by a nimble-fingered dressmaker, who stayed at a house for weeks in order to fit out different members of the family.

"I shall see that you have a rose-bud sash and new slippers, at any rate," Thankful's grandmother said with determination, and she was better than her word.

The slippers were of fine morocco leather, crossed over the ankles and tied with ribbons. The new sash quite transformed her old best India muslin, and when her hair was brushed smooth and glistening and an old blue enamel locket of her mother's loaned for the occasion, her grandmother said she would do, though it was not what she could have wished. She didn't know how they would ever get rid of all those dreadful freckles. I thought no one was going to pay any heed to my appearance and I grew quite worried. But at the last moment Little Thankful found a piece that had been snipped off the sash. This she wrapped about me shawl fashion and she pulled my beads out to show as much as possible. So off we set for the party.

The Pryces' house was only a few doors distant; a maid was dispatched with us, and soon we were in another fine brick house and our wraps being laid on an enormous canopied bed with a great many other little cloaks and bonnets. Such a babble of voices came up from below stairs. It sounded to me like the noise of the baby crows in the old pine, and this put me in a less happy mood to go down to it. But down we went, Little Thankful holding me in one hand and clinging to the balustrade with the other (she still found it strange to go up or down stairs, since the house in India had been built, native fashion, all on one floor). A large lady in still more rustling silks met us and kissed the child warmly.

"Ah," said she, peering down at her, "I must take a good look at you to see which side of the house you favor."

"I don't want to look like any house," said Little Thankful, who was beginning to feel less shy after being ashore a whole day, "and I mean to wear a nose-ring when I grow up."

The lady looked very much startled at this, and I heard her repeating it to another lady later on and adding that she did not envy the old people the life she was going to lead them.

We were now conducted to a very large room, which seemed completely filled with little girls in ballooning frocks and gay sashes. They looked like a flock of tropical butterflies, I thought, with their bright bows, their starched ruffles, lacy pantalettes, and shining curls. I was enchanted by the sight and I had no idea they were not as charming in manner as in appearance. In this I was mistaken. Indeed, I underwent such a shock at that party that I have not had quite the same faith in human nature since. For no sooner were the grown-up people out of the way than the little girls gathered about us and began to pass remarks upon Little Thankful's appearance and mine. They tittered and whispered things to each other behind their hands in a way that was anything but reassuring. Perhaps they meant no real harm, but certainly they did nothing to make us feel at ease in their midst.

"If that is the way they dress in India, I shall certainly never go there," said one pert young Miss in flowered dimity.

"What makes you have so many freckles?" asked another, peering at her very rudely, "and why don't you wear curls and ruffles all the way up your skirts?"

This to Little Thankful, who had been led to fancy herself perfect in every detail! I could not but feel sorry for her during this trying ordeal, for she was quite unequal to answering their jibes. She continued to stare back at the children as if they were strange animals into whose claws she had fallen. I could not blame her, and I felt almost relieved when after a time they caught sight of me and began to poke fun at my appearance instead. "At least I am going to be some help to her," I thought. "She will be grateful to me when we are home again."

The things those children said about me! It would depress me too much even now to repeat them all, but they left me scarcely a shred of comfort. If I had not been a doll of experience and some poise, I doubt if I should ever have recovered from that half-hour of criticism. According to those little girls, I was "an ugly old thing," "a perfect fright," and I looked as if I "came out of the Ark."

But what hurt me most of all was when one young lady said that I looked as if the cat had fished me out of the dump-heap. Of course, I had not been so foolish as to suppose my experiences in salt water, fire, and the tropics had left me untouched. But somehow I had not realized that their ravages were so apparent. I knew my complexion had suffered somewhat, but then, so had other people's. At any rate, this remark went deep, though I am happy to say that no one would have guessed it to look at me. No, I was one to remain true to my type and pleasant expression.

The little girls now began to bring out their own dolls, and I must admit in all truth that I did not make much of a showing among them. In the first place, my size was against me, for these were all of more imposing stature, and many of them had beautifully glazed china heads. There were even some exquisite wax beauties with real hair and wide, glass eyes. I was the only wooden one in the lot, and even the most simply dressed of them all looked like a princess beside my modest attire. I thought if only Little Thankful would show them more corals, this might help, but her one idea was to get me out of sight as speedily as possible.

At last, the children were summoned to supper in the dining-room beyond. All the dolls were hastily heaped upon a big sofa before the fire. I found myself with a china lady on one side and an enormous wax beauty of dazzling complexion on the other. It was a very trying position to be in. No sign passed between us there, but I felt their eyes regarding me with disapproval.

I did not make much of a showing among the other dolls.

"Still, beauty is not everything in this world," I told myself.

Just at that moment I could not but feel it was a very great help, indeed; nevertheless I determined to do my best no matter what might happen, in order that Little Thankful should have no cause to feel ashamed of me. Ah, how little did I guess the scheme that was even then stirring in her mind as she sat at the long table with the others!

And now comes the unbelievable part of this whole episode. It pains me to tell it, but told it must be.

When the lighted birthday cake was brought in and all the children got up from their places to crowd about and blow the candles out, Little Thankful contrived to slip unnoticed from the room. Quick as a wink she ran in and over to our sofa. I thought she was coming to fetch me in with her to share in the festivities. But, no, indeed, far different thoughts were prompting her!

Before I could take in what had happened, she had seized me and thrust me with all her strength into the narrow corner where the back, arm, and seat of the sofa all fitted together. I was really too big to go in, but she was determined, and her fingers forced and pushed me out of sight. The sofa was done in horsehair, which scratched me cruelly as I went in. Had I been made of anything but stout ash wood, I feel sure I should have snapped in two, but somehow or other I survived. Once I was past the edge of the seat, there was slightly more room, a sort of corner behind the framework and upholstery, of the size a mouse might use to set up housekeeping in before his family grew too numerous.

In a daze of despair I lay there and heard Little Thankful running back to the other room. It was not possible, I thought, that she could have deserted me, and after I had taken so much of the criticism upon my own person when things were going their worst. It is a bitter thing, indeed, to realize that those one holds dear are ashamed of one. I think I have never suffered more in my life than when I realized what had happened. Even later on, when the children came to collect their dolls from the sofa to go home, and I heard them bewailing the fact that my beautiful wax neighbor's face had started to run from being too near the fire, even then I could scarcely take the satisfaction in this that I should formerly have taken. No doll but must have felt miserable under the circumstances.

## CHAPTER X
# In Which I Am Rescued and Hear Adelina Patti

I do not know how long I remained in my horsehair home, but after my cramped stay there I have always held with the saying that one can adapt oneself to any situation. Of course, I grew tired lying in such a small space, with my legs folded over myself just as I had been thrust so rudely, but that discomfort was less hard to bear than the humiliation I suffered.

Soon after the birthday party, the sofa was sent up to the attic to make room for a new one of rosewood and brocade. I heard a long discussion about it from my hiding-place and I only wished the old one was to be done over so that I might be released. Instead, I felt it being hoisted on the shoulders of a couple of men, who carried it up several flights of stairs. After that there was little to relieve the monotony of my days. Moths and an occasional nibbling mouse were my only visitors, and even they soon became discouraged by the stiffness of the horsehair.

All through this trying period of my life I had much time for reflection. I could not feel that Little Thankful had benefited greatly from all the hymns, texts, and other religious instructions she had received, if she could abandon me at the first shade of criticism. I have no doubt that she had explained away my disappearance and that her kind grandparents had bought her the first wax doll she fancied.

"True worth counts for little," I sighed to myself in the dust and discomfort of my little hole. "It is a hard world for those of us who are not able to keep our complexions."

So I reasoned, sometimes trying to solace myself by repeating all the hymns and texts I could remember, especially those dealing with the fleeting and the changefulness of human affections.

I had plenty of time for this during my years in the horse-hair sofa, for when I was at last taken from my hiding-place I found that the little girl in whose honor the party had been given was now grown up and married. It was to one of her younger cousins that I was to belong. I am happy to say that she much preferred me to the rag and china children she already possessed.

My rescue happened in this way: Sometimes a group of children would visit the attic on days when I could hear the rain pelting down on the tin roof just above. I always looked forward to those days and to hearing the voices and laughing and chatter, even though I was always more lonely after the feet had gone tramping down the attic stairs again when the super bell was rung below. One day, more children came than usual, boys and girls together.

"Let's play train on the sofa," one of them suggested, and soon they were all crowded on it.

At that time I had no idea what trains were, though I was to learn about them as soon as I emerged once more into the outside world, for they were taking the place of the stagecoach everywhere. Well, those children did their best to be as noisy as the loudest steam engine. They bounced up and down above me and beat their feet against the framework till I expected us all to collapse together. But the old sofa must have been as stoutly built as if it, too, were of mountain-ash wood. Just as I was almost wishing it would go, so that I should be set free at last, even though in splinters, I felt a hand thrust into the opening beside me. Imagine my suspense lest the fingers should be withdrawn before they found me, and imagine my joy when I felt them actually closing round my waist!

The next thing I knew the children's faces were all bent over me, and they were poking and peering with great curiosity.

"Why, it's a doll!" they cried, "a funny wooden doll! How ever do you suppose it got into that old sofa?"

They trooped down with it to show the various grown-up members of the household. But none of them could think how I had come there, and the oldest cousin, who might have remembered me from her party, was living away off in Kansas, a place I had never even heard of before.

So I was adopted by Clarissa Pryce, in whose care I spent some of the pleasantest years of my life. It was a less adventurous period, for me, but one in which I learned much that has been profitable to me later. Indeed, I should not now know how to hold my pen and write these words as I do if I had not been Clarissa's desk companion at the little dame school she attended just round the corner.

Clarissa was a quiet child, older by some years than my other owners, for she celebrated her tenth birthday soon after I was found. She was a frail little girl, less given to games and romping than her brothers and sisters and the cousins from over the way who used to join them so often. She had a small, grave face with a pointed chin, gray eyes, and softest brown hair, that seldom became tumbled about like the other children's. Her hands were very gentle and she was far more skillful with needle and thread than either of my other young mistresses. This was a good thing, for I had certainly never been more in want of clothes. The very day she found me she began to replenish my wardrobe, so of course it was not long before she discovered my chemise and name.

"Thee must have been thought highly of, Hitty," she said, "to wear coral beads and thy name in cross-stitch, too."

I was a little puzzled by her talk at first, till I learned that they were Quakers, who always called each other "thee." So when I heard her address me so, I felt pleased, because I knew this meant that I was an outsider no longer but a real member of the Pryce family. Clarissa's mother was a little doubtful about my being allowed to keep my coral beads. She dressed in plain colors herself and did not hold with wearing jewelry and "furbelows," as she called them. However, when Clarissa pleaded and she saw how becoming they were to me, she decided that I might keep them on if Clarissa did not draw attention to them too frequently and if the neck was made high enough to keep them from being too conspicuous. Clarissa was very conscientious about this, though she often looked at them to make sure they were there. She was never allowed a locket or bright colors, herself; blue ribbons to tie under the chin from her best leghorn were the nearest she ever came to finery.

However, if my clothes were less gay, at least I had more of them, and each of my two outfits could be taken on and off. One of these was brown sprigs on buff calico to be worn six days of the week, and the other was a pearl-gray silk, made in true Quaker fashion, with a fine white fichu crossed in front, lawn cap, and all, for First Day, as the Pryces called Sunday.

"Now she looks like a true Friend," said Clarissa, when I was finally arrayed in it. It was some time before I understood that Quakers mean something a little different from the rest of the world when they use the word. With them it is another name for people who believe as they do.

"Yes," agreed Mrs. Pryce, "I could almost expect her to be moved by the spirit to speak in Meeting, though thee must not take her there to see."

So I realized that people had not changed in their opinions about dolls attending church, as they had in other ways—in their methods of traveling, for instance, or the way they dressed. I noticed a good many changes in this line as I went about the streets in Clarissa's hands or, from the broad window sill that faced the street, watched the people pass. Skirts were fuller than they had been in the old days. Now they had wire hoops inside to make them stand out all round, and the waists fitted so tightly that I wondered some of the ladies managed to draw any breath at all. Clarissa's older sister Ruth used to sigh as she saw these elegant costumes and was heard to wish that she had not been born a Quaker. She was a beautiful girl of eighteen then, with black eyes and hair and very pink cheeks, but far too given to the vanities of this world, as her mother often warned her.

Ruth was very kind about saving scraps of silk and muslin for my clothes and in helping Clarissa to make them up for me. Indeed, the doll house was her idea, for she found the wooden box in the attic, cleared it out, and showed how it could be made into a delightful one-room home for me. Clarissa was enchanted and soon had the sides papered and a smaller box covered for me for a bench. A cousin who was visiting the family bought her a little desk with a lid that lifted exactly as Clarissa's own did over at the dame school. I could now sit on my bench before my own desk for all the world as if I were studying. Indeed, Clarissa cut me tiny sheets of paper the size of a postage stamp, and her brother Will made me a quill pen out of a feather shed by a neighbor's parrot. This was a green so bright, with a touch of scarlet thrown in, that I feared Mrs. Pryce would decide it was much too gaudy for a Quaker doll. However, I think she did not object, because the parrot had been endowed at birth with such colors.

"Nature need not be improved upon," she used to say, which made me wonder what she would have thought of the way the savages on the Island decorated themselves.

So I spent many happy, studious days in my little room with its appropriate furnishings, and later that winter I acquired a braided rug of proper proportions and a china dog to lie upon it.

However, I am getting ahead of myself, for a good deal happened between the month of August, when I came out of the attic, and the beginnings of the next year. It was in late October, I think, that we began to hear rumors about the coming of Adelina Patti. Everyone was talking about her. It was rumored she had a throat like a bird because she could do such intricate trills and reach such high notes. She was not much older than Ruth and had been the sensation of New York. This was to be her only concert in Philadelphia before she sailed away to Europe to sing before Kings and Queens. Soon, at school, at tea parties, and even on street corners the one absorbing topic of conversation came to be whether or not

I could now sit on my bench before my own desk.

one was going to be lucky enough to hear Adelina Patti sing.

Ruth wanted to go more than anything else she could think of, but her parents felt it an extravagance far too great and an event far too worldly to be considered. As for Clarissa, she never even asked, being a practical child and knowing quite well how such a request would be received. But she kept her ears ready to gather all bits of news she could about the young singer and even cut a picture of her from a paper that some one gave her and pasted it on the wall of my house. I became as familiar with the features of Adelina Patti at nineteen as if they had been my own. I could not say I thought so much of them, but then I knew that it was her throat that mattered and what came out of it.

The morning of the concert all Philadelphia seemed to wear a look of excited curiosity. Even the houses appeared to be waiting to hear what should be said of the concert, and at school, where Clarissa carried me to sit in a far corner under her desk lid, I heard nothing but whisperings from the little girls who were lucky enough to be going. There were only three who were, and they could easily be distinguished from the rest because their hair was screwed up in curl papers in readiness for the evening. It was chatter, chatter, chatter about it all through recess and whisperings behind books till school let out for the day.

On the way home, a boy joined us and walked with Clarissa to carry her books, as he often did. He was a round-faced German boy who lived not far away. His name was Paul Schneider, and I had always liked him, though some of the girls at school made fun of his rather shabby clothes and his slow foreign way of talking. His father kept a baker shop on another street. Many would not walk with him for this reason.

"You want to go to de concert?" I heard him ask her unexpectedly. "You vould like to hear Adelina Patti sing?"

I could hardly believe my ears. Yes, I heard Clarissa say, she would like nothing better, but of course she could not go.

"Bud you can go," he told her, his round face smiling with satisfaction. "I vill take you mit me."

I felt Clarissa shiver a little.

"But how could you?" she asked incredulously. "It costs dollars and dollars to go and all the tickets have been sold for weeks."

"I do nod need tickets," he told her, "begauze my Uncle Hans plays his flute and he vill brink us in vere does players come. I go vid him oftentimes."

Poor Clarissa was all a-tremble by this time. I knew what must be going on in her mind. A spot of pink showed in either cheek as she listened to more plans from Paul. I remembered as well as she that her father and mother were going out to cousins for supper and the evening. They would not be back till late. It would be only too easy for her to slip out after she was supposed to be in her room asleep and meet Paul at the corner. The more he told her about how pleasant it would be, the harder it became for her to help joining in the plan. I think it must have been because she was usually such a good, obedient child that, once she listened to temptation, it was harder for her to resist. So she promised she would be ready to go with him and his uncle at the time he said.

All that afternoon I sat staring at the picture of Adelina Patti and wondering whether Clarissa would take me, too. When she came in before supper after seeing her parents drive off, her face was so flushed and the pupils of her eyes so big and dark, I knew she meant to keep her word to Paul Schneider. Presently, I felt a guilty thrill clear down to my bottom pegs, for I saw she was getting out my dress from its box. Off came my calico and on went the silk. The white lawn scratched my neck a little, but I was willing to let it, for I wished to look my best. I was glad when I felt her pull out my corals so that they would show more than her mother would have thought proper.

Things could not have worked out better for us if they had been planned. Ruth hurried the younger children through their supper because she had been told to see them in bed before she went over to spend the evening with a friend. She was resigned now about not going to the concert and determined to have as much fun as possible elsewhere. So she hustled Will off to his books and the younger boys into bed.

"Thee may stay up till nine tonight," she told Clarissa, "but mind thee folds thy clothes neatly over the chair."

She was off without waiting for any answer, and no sooner was she round the corner than Clarissa sped up to her little room. She set me down on her chest of drawers while with trembling but swift fingers she got out her best gray merino with the scalloped skirt and sleeves and put it on. Her best pantalettes and slippers with crisscross ribbons looked very well with it, and finally, in a burst of recklessness, she went into her sister's room and took a blue satin sash from her upper drawer. It had been a gift and Ruth herself was seldom allowed to wear it. All this took place quickly and without the least noise. By the time the November twilight had fallen she was ready and slipping out of a side door in her brown cloak and hood. And I was under the cloak going to hear Adelina Patti, too. No one saw us go; the servants were busy in the kitchen, Will was bent over his Latin, and the two little boys indulging in a game upstairs that would never have been allowed with the older members of the household about.

It was a chill fall evening. The lamplighter had made his rounds early and all the lamps looked like tall ghosts on their posts. I could feel Clarissa's heart beating even faster than it had before and her breath was very short as she sped along by the familiar houses. Suppose, I felt sure she was thinking, that some neighbor should call out and ask where she was going all by herself at such an hour. But no one did. Either all the neighbors were eating supper or else they were getting ready for the concert themselves.

Paul and his Uncle Hans were at the next corner. Paul looked quite unlike his usual self done up in a big plaid shawl of his father's. He and Clarissa took hands and hurried along beside Uncle Hans, who was very fat and looked more so in a great coat with many capes. He carried a black leather case carefully under one arm. This, Paul explained, was his flute and would be all jointed and put together when he got to the Hall. Clarissa had to run most of the way and her cape blew about, which gave me a chance to see what was going on around me. The two children hardly talked at all, as they needed all their breath to keep pace with the man's strides. They were late, apparently, and he feared it would be hard to pass the two in if all the musicians had got there ahead of him. Finally, we turned into a street packed with carriages of every description. There were many lights and much commotion about several great doors where people were crowding.

"Ach!" said Uncle Hans under his breath, "such a sight, and until it begins still an hour yet."

He told each of his two charges to hold firmly to one of his coat tails and do as he said. They followed him to a smaller door on a sort of alleyway. This, also, was packed, but with men whom our guide hailed in German. Most of them carried bulky instruments and we had a time crowding past the one who bore a bass viol on his back. At last we were inside and standing in a queer open space they called "the wings," though I could see no reason for giving it such a name. Uncle Hans spoke to a man named Ole who seemed to be in charge, and after a little conversation he nodded his head and beckoned to Clarissa and Paul.

"I will look out for you two," he said. "You shall not miss nothing."

The musicians were all getting seated outside on what I later discovered was the stage, but with the curtains still down I could not then see it. They had their instruments out now and were tuning them up as they talked and turned over their sheets of music. We could see Uncle Hans a long way off with his silver flute laid along his lips. Paul knew many of the other players and told Clarissa who they were, but there was too much noise for me to hear much of what he said. Clarissa seemed to have given herself up completely to the joy of the evening. Only once do I remember her having any compunctions at being there and then she reminded herself and me that she had not, like Ruth, asked her mother to let her hear Adelina Patti.

"So of course I am not really disobeying," she said aloud.

Paul Schneider was too busy telling her how many lamps

there would be shining the other side of the curtain when it went up to question her, and soon there was too much excitement going on all round us to think of anything else. Other people were waiting nearby, but our friend Ole was as good as his word. He stood by our sides and let no one crowd in front of us. Now we began to hear the babble of voices beyond the curtain.

"It's a big house tonight," he told us. "I guess there never were such a lot of people in this Hall since it was built—not since Jenny Lind sang in it once, anyway. I expect Patti'll be just as famous some day, if she is only nineteen."

Well, finally the time came round, our friend pulled at some ropes hanging beside him, and the curtains parted the other side of the musicians. The lights were even brighter than Paul had said they would be, the crystal drops from the chandeliers gave out rainbow colors, and hundreds upon hundreds of faces showed, stretching away like a meadow of daisies in June. A gallery above that was thronged till there seemed not an inch of room left. All the time the rustlings and babblings kept up. Clarissa complained of being hot and Ole took her cape and Paul's shawl and put them on a high stool. Then he lifted Clarissa onto it. She kept me held tight, and we had a fine view of the musicians' heads bending over strings and flutes as the music began to rise up till the air all round us was filled with it.

Although I cannot truthfully say that I am musically inclined, and it has not been my fortune to move in musical circles, still I shall never forget that night or the beautiful sounds that came from between the lips of the scrawny, dark-eyed girl in the elaborately ruffled dress. We saw her being led out of her dressing-room. The people watching with us were packed so thick that a big man with many gold chains across his chest and a gold-topped cane had to push them aside to make a path for her to walk through. Then he went with her onto the stage and escorted her to a platform which stood in the midst of all the musicians. They were playing when she came out, but once the audience caught sight of her they began such a clapping and hallooing and stamping that no one would have guessed the men were playing except that their fingers moved up and down the strings or little holes in their flutes and the bows dipped and sent out flashes from their tips.

I must confess that there is no music which seems to me to compare with that of a good Swiss music box; still, I shall always maintain that no one has ever sung as Adelina Patti did that night in Philadelphia. She seemed not to mind the people at all. She stood on her wooden block there among the musicians and when some one tossed a rose at her feet she stooped and picked it up as calmly as if all the hundreds of eyes had not been fastened upon her. And then she began to sing.

"An angel from heaven, dot's vot she is," sobbed an old German woman who stood behind us, when the first number was finished.

But that was not my idea of Adelina Patti at all. She was much more like a brown thrush or a meadow lark to my way of thinking. In one song she did actually pretend to be one. There were all manner of little trills and chirrups in it and sometimes she would make echoes of what she had just sung before. People went wild after that one. They cried her name again and again and a word called "encore," which Paul explained to Clarissa meant "again." She did it for them several times and at last the musicians had to stop playing because the people kept throwing flowers at her. There were far too many now for her to pick them up. Besides, she must keep bowing and smiling over and over as the people clapped and cheered and crowded close to see her. Those behind her were just as excited as those in front. They pressed nearer and nearer till they were actually out on the stage.

Somehow or other, I am not sure when or how, Clarissa got off the stool. After that it was impossible not to be swept along with the crowd. She managed to keep close to Paul and to hold me tight, as we were pushed and jostled this way and that. Clarissa hardly looked like the same child, her cheeks were so flushed, her eyes were so bright, and her brown hair tumbled about her shoulders in anything but its usual smoothness. Her hands were so hot that my lawn fichu became wilted where she clutched me, and still we went on with the rest till we were out upon the big stage ourselves under the lights and in plain view of all the faces looking up from below.

How we got so far out I do not know, but I suddenly discovered that we were close to the platform on which the singer was standing. The musicians and their shining instruments were all around us. I remember my surprise to see that fiddle bows were not made of whalebone, as I had always supposed, but that their white part was innumerable hairs as fine and smooth-looking as glass. The next thing I knew, we were on the platform, too!

But not the whole crowd, only Clarissa and I. One of the

musicians, I think, must have lifted her up there beside the great singer. If it had happened less suddenly, I might have been frightened. As it was, I felt nothing but great interest in all that was going on. Such a tumult of cheers and hand-clappings as there was, too! Now that we were so close to Adelina Patti I could see that she looked like her picture, and that she was not so much taller than Clarissa. Her dark hair was braided elaborately with colored ribbons and crossed and recrossed about her head after some old foreign fashion, her eyes were shining like blackberries after rain, and her throat seemed much too small for all that music. She smiled down at us pleasantly and reached out a slim brown hand to take Clarissa's. Now it happened that I was in the nearer one and just for a second or so Clarissa was so flustered it didn't occur to her to change me to the other one. I think she must have been suddenly overcome by all the faces looking at us and the fact that the blue sash was all askew. But she changed me over to her other hand finally and put hers in Patti's while people cheered and pelted us with more flowers.

What occurred after that is all a confused jumble in my mind. Adelina Patty was borne away through the crowd, and still people streamed after her, eager to catch a glimpse of her face or one of her flowers or ready to tear the very ruffles of her dress. It was no place for a frail little girl of ten and a doll of my size, and for a few minutes I wondered if we would come through the crush at all. The stiff, ballooning hoop skirts all around did not help matters any. It was like being caught in a close-pressing forest of silk, satin, and crinoline. Clarissa had lost Paul completely. She could scarcely breathe with so many large bodies packed about her. I began to fear she would smother, for I could feel her struggling to get her breath and calling for Ole and Uncle Hans. Any minute I expected to be dashed from her hands and trampled under so many feet. It seemed a long time that we were there, but I suppose it could not have been more than ten or fifteen minutes before Ole found us and managed to drag us to safety and a place where Clarissa could breathe again.

"No place for children when people go off their heads," he said, carrying us in his arms to a little door, and none too soon, either, for word had just been passed round that Adelina Patti would go out to her carriage presently and the crowd swarmed thicker than ever over the stage and into the wings.

Uncle Hans and Paul were waiting by the door and they lost no time in getting out of the alleyway. It was no use even trying to look for Clarissa's cloak and hood or Paul's shawl. Uncle Hans wrapped a big woolen scarf about her as best he could and off we started for home.

"Vell," he said as we reached our corner, "you don't forget de time you hear Patti, I tink. Dere iss plenty people wish dat dey vas you."

But Clarissa was too spent and shivering to say more than a brief thanks and good-night. She was just turning in to go to her own side door, when there was a sound of voices at the front steps, lights showed in the hall, and her father and mother were hurrying out to meet us.

"Oh, Mother," I heard Clarissa say, "thee must not let me in till thee hears where Hitty and I have been."

Then she began to cry and her teeth to chatter so that her words all ran together with gasps and sobs between. But it seemed that her mother and father knew without her telling them that she had been to the concert. By a strange coincidence, they had been there themselves along with the cousins to whose house they had gone for supper. Apparently, their evening had been almost as full of surprises as ours—the greatest being when they had seen their daughter appear on the stage beside the great prima donna. I heard Mrs. Pryce telling a neighbor all about it next day and reading a piece from the paper that mentioned Clarissa as a "little Quaker maid" who was given a share in the demonstration.

"I should not have been able to listen to a note Patti sang had I known Clarissa was in that terrible mob," she went on, "and you can imagine her father's feelings and mine when we saw her up there under all the lights. He tried to go and get her, but no one could move for the crowds."

"If she were mine," said the neighbor, who was a shrewish widow and far from a favorite with the boys and girls on the street, "I'd give her something besides Patti to remember the evening by."

I knew what she meant and so did Mrs. Pryce. But I think she felt Clarissa was upset enough, so she contented herself with keeping her in bed a few days in case she might be laid up with a cold, and helping her repair all damage done to her best dress and Ruth's sash. As for the brown cape and hood, no sign of them was ever seen again, though Uncle Hans and Ole swore they had looked everywhere.

## CHAPTER XI
# In Which I Sit for My Daguerreotype and Meet a Poet

There are two events of that time that stand out with particular clearness. The first was when Clarissa's grandfather decided that he wanted to have her daguerreotype taken. This was a form of photography very popular at that time and, indeed, one to which I am to this day very partial. These pictures were taken with a camera on small glass plates which were later colored appropriately and fixed in miniature black cases with red plush and gold-leaf borders inside. Ruth had hers done on her eighteenth birthday and I have no doubt Clarissa would have had to wait as long for hers had her grandfather not intervened. He had a special affection in his heart for Clarissa because she resembled a little sister of his who had died many years before. She, too, had been named Clarissa, and Grandfather Pryce had a beautiful little miniature of her in a locket which he sometimes showed us when Clarissa took me to his big house for First Day dinner. He wanted one of his grandchild at the same age.

So one day Clarissa was dressed in her best, a brown cashmere, this time, for the gray merino was never quite what it had been before the Patti concert, and off we went to the Daguerreotype-Artist's studio. Clarissa's grandfather was a kindly and talkative old gentleman, and we kept meeting so many people he knew along the way that it seemed we should never get to the place before the sun went down. However, we managed to, and soon we were opening one small case after another, while the Artist showed us all the different ways he could pose his subjects.

Fortunately, Clarissa was a quiet child, who minded less than most the moments of sitting perfectly still without moving so much as an eyelash. As for me, this was no hardship at all. I pictured how fine it would be to see myself against the crimson cloth that covered a small table upon which Clarissa rested the hand that held me. I could hardly wait to see the finished pictures when we went a few days later to call for them. The Artist wished to see Clarissa again before he put in the color, as Grandfather Pryce impressed upon him the importance of making her hair and eyes the right shade and not putting too much pink on her cheeks.

Well, you can imagine my feelings when the pictures were shown and it turned out that I did not appear in them at all. The plates all ended before I began. It was very disappointing and nothing could make Clarissa resigned to it.

"I wanted Hitty to be in it, too," was all she would say over and over.

In vain the Artist tried to explain and her grandfather to reason with her. They were such excellent likenesses of her, it seemed doubtful if the Artist could do so well again. Finally, he had an idea.

"Since it is my fault," he said, bowing in a queer foreign way he had, "that Mademoiselle your granddaughter is not satisfied, perhaps she will permit the doll to sit for me alone?"

Clarissa was enchanted, and I felt myself almost overpowered by the honor. It was lucky that my pleasant expression was so firmly fixed, as otherwise I think I might not have managed to keep it during the ordeal. The Artist took as much pains with me as if I had been one of his most distinguished subjects. Unfortunately, I was not wearing my best clothes this second time. But Clarissa hovered over me, arranging my skirts and pulling out my beads, while the Artist brought out a tiny jug with roses on it and some orange berries to put behind me. These were very like mountain-ash berries and I considered it a most fortunate coincidence that they were to be in my background.

"They set off her brunette type charmingly," said the Artist, as he peered through his camera box on its three legs. "What is it that you call her, Mademoiselle?"

So Clarissa told him my name and that I had come from the inside of a horsehair sofa and had been to hear Adelina Patti sing.

"Experience as well as character," said the Artist, "ah, yes, it is easily seen that she has both. I shall try to do her justice."

Then he put his head under a black cloth and slid a plate into the box.

"Now, Mademoiselle Hitty," he said from under the black folds, "I shall have to request that you keep perfectly still for one moment, and a pleasant expression, if you please."

Well, no sitter could have been more obliging than I. He seemed appreciative of this and told Clarissa and her grandfather that he could not have asked for a better subject.

"She shall come with the others tomorrow," he promised, as he bowed us out, "to Mademoiselle with my compliments."

He was as good as his word. The next night Grandfather

Pryce came over after supper with the pictures in a packet. He was smiling so broadly that I knew he was pleased with them, and all the family gathered round to pass judgment. Clarissa's were pronounced excellent likenesses, but as for mine, it had turned out so well that it had to be passed round and round and the case opened and closed so many times I was afraid it would be worn out the very first evening. I could hardly believe my eyes when I saw myself there in the gilt-edged oval, my buff sprigged skirts neatly spread about me, a scallop or two of petticoat showing beneath, my feet and hands as wooden as life, and my expression as pleasant as the day the Old Peddler had given it to me so long ago in Maine. Best of all, the Artist had touched the flowers on the mug with pink, and the berries with green and orange, while my own corals were as bright as I could wish.

I often wonder what has become of that daguerreotype. Miss Hunter would certainly carry on if she ever saw it. Even then, before I was considered an antique and people began collecting daguerreotypes, it was displayed as a great curiosity. Dolls had been taken in them, of course, but always with their young mistresses. I have yet to hear of one sitting alone for her portrait.

The next most important event which I recall of this time was the visit of Mr. John Greenleaf Whittier, the poet. He was already a familiar name in the Pryce household, being the most famous Quaker of his day as well as a friend of the family. The occasion of his coming was that he was to read a poem at a large meeting being held to protest against Slavery. Like nearly all Quakers, the Pryces felt that all the slaves in the South should be freed. They read a book called "Uncle Tom's

Cabin" aloud and I must say that what I heard of it did upset me a good deal, especially the part about whippings and when bloodhounds chased poor Eliza over the ice cakes. Indeed, this chapter so affected Clarissa's tender heart that her mother said it was better for her not to hear any more, since it kept them up nights trying to console the child for her bad dreams. To this day I do not know exactly what all the trouble was about, but I do know that the meeting was to be very important and that Grandfather Pryce was to introduce the Poet.

He thought it would be nice for Clarissa to learn one of his poems to say to him. I could not help feeling that a poet might like to hear some other poem instead, since from what I heard I gathered that it is quite hard work to make the right words rhyme when they should. But of course I had nothing to say about it and Clarissa was set down to memorize one called "Telling the Bees." It had some quite pretty parts, but I thought it a sad song for a little girl to learn, because it was about a man coming back to a farmhouse and finding that the lady he loved had died and the chore-girl was draping all the beehives in crape and singing. But Clarissa was very conscientious and by the day he was to arrive she knew all the verses by heart.

From a second-story window Clarissa and I saw Mr. Whittier drive up. Her father and grandfather were showing him up the steps. I cannot say that there was anything about him to make you know he was a poet. I had on my gray dress in his honor and when Ruth came to fetch us down to the parlor I must confess to several shivers in my pegs.

But Mr. Whittier proved to be a thin, very kindly man. He did not talk in rhymes, as I had feared he might, and he smiled as often as anybody else behind his grayish beard. Clarissa said the *bee-poem* through right away as soon as they had shaken hands. He listened to it very carefully and thanked her when she had finished.

"Thee has a sweet voice, my dear," he said. "May thee never have cause to raise it in protest."

I was just beginning to feel rather left out of the conversation, when Mr. Whittier caught sight of me. Clarissa needed no further encouragement. Soon she was running off to get my daguerreotype, leaving me on the poet's knee. The fact that I was in Quaker dress pleased him. He examined me with grave pleasure. He listened, too, to all that Clarissa could tell him of my history.

"Hitty," he repeated thoughtfully after her, "a plain name but not without charm."

He also remarked that he had never seen a more tranquil brow than mine. He would have said more, perhaps, had they not been summoned to supper.

Clarissa and I were not allowed to go to the meeting, as were Ruth and William. I think Mr. Whittier must have felt sorry about this. At all events, upon parting next day, he left a folded piece of paper in Clarissa's hands. When this was read it proved to be a poem, written in the poet's own hand *and* about me. It was called, if I remember rightly, "Lines to a Quaker Doll of Philadelphia," and it began in the following manner:

> *These verses are in praise of thee,*
> *Though finger's length of modesty,*
> *Whose tranquil brow and dress of gray*
> *Become thee more than bright array*

I am sorry I cannot remember it all, for even Mr. and Mrs. Pryce were impressed. They kept it in the parlor what-not along with my daguerreotype. I wish I knew what has become of it. I fear it must have been lost, since it never seems to be mentioned, not even in the "Complete Poems" of Mr. John Greenleaf Whittier.

And now comes a time that is strange to remember, in which things became so confused in my memory that I scarcely know what to say of it. I do not know when I began to hear about soldiers and fighting and speeches by a man named Abraham Lincoln, who was called President. To this day I am not clear what it was all about, only I know that "Uncle Tom's Cabin" and Topsy and Eva and the bloodhounds were all mixed up in it and that the Pryce family wore very long faces and went to more meetings than before. Quakers did not believe that anything was worth killing other people about. Still, they said they believed Mr. Lincoln was right in holding that the Southern States had no right to set up a government of their own.

Quite well do I remember the day old Grandfather Pryce walked in with a very grave face and his cane shaking in his hand.

"Sarah," he said to Clarissa's mother, who met him in the hall, "it has come to War."

From my place on the window sill where I had been left I heard him say it and saw the tears roll down his cheeks as he read her the call for volunteers.

After that there was a different air about the whole city, and though I lived in a Quaker household, which was not sending men away to fight, still we all felt it, too. Many a time I have sat on the front steps or looked from a window with Clarissa as long blue lines of men marched by, muskets on their shoulders, packs on their backs, and their feet all moving together like the spokes of wheels, till it made one dizzy to look.

Sometimes Paul Schneider came and sat beside Clarissa on our steps and told her which regiments they were and where they had come from. Once he read off a name that startled me.

"Look," he said, pointing to the letters on a flag, "the twelfth Maine infantry division. They've come a long way."

I thought of the Preble house on the road between Bath and Portland and I knew better than any just how far they had come. Ruth felt more interest in those from nearer by. Many of the boys she knew were training in camp. She used to knit socks and write letters to those she knew best. There was one, a pleasant, round-faced fellow named John Norton, who sent her a button from his first uniform and also his picture—a funny little tintype affair. I noticed that she treasured both very carefully. Ruth was graver and quieter than she had been a year ago, and no wonder, for before very long it turned out that she had promised John Norton to marry him when he came back from fighting with General McClellan. When she wasn't around, her father and mother discussed it very soberly and told each other she would be lucky if young Norton ever came back alive.

As time went on, and the papers kept printing lists of men who had been killed and news about campaigns and charges and camps, I found Clarissa paid less attention to me than of old. It was not that she wasn't still fond of me, but like the older members of the family she must help in all sorts of ways she had not known before. Several of the servants were dismissed. There was more sewing and housework to be done, and in odd moments and each evening all the women would gather and scrape lint from the cotton which was to make bandages for the wounded. It was not the easiest work. Fingers became stiff and sore in a very short time. I sat in my little house on a corner of the living-room mantelpiece and watched them at it. It seemed too bad that I could not help, too. My wooden hands would have proved excellent in the scraping line, not nearly so easily tired as Clarissa's. But no one thought to set me at it.

Now the two youngest boys played at soldiers all day in the yard and no one in the family thought to reprove them. Will declared he would run away and join a regiment as soon as he was a year older. Ruth's cheeks were not so red as they had been. She spent all her time scraping lint and rolling bandages and waiting for letters from the front. One day she got one that said John Norton was seriously wounded from a shot in the leg. Clarissa told Paul and all the children in the neighborhood about it.

"He'll walk mit a wooden leg vhen he come back," said Paul.

"Maybe he won't ever come back," said Clarissa. "She wears the button he gave her on a ribbon round her neck and she sleeps with his tintype under her pillow. I saw her put it there the other night."

"Vell, so she should," declared Paul, "she has promised she vill marry him."

As time went on, I came more and more to look on at the doings of the Pryce household rather than to take part in them. Clarissa gave away the rag and china babies, but she kept me, even though she declared she was twelve now and too old for dolls. I lost track of time, and the sound of drums and fifes in the street outside stirred me no more than the ticking of the clock in the hall.

I told myself that when the War was over everything would be as it had been before. But I knew better than to believe this, for a doll of my experience has learned that nothing can ever be just the same once there has been change of any sort.

A letter came one day from John Norton, who was better and being cared for in a Southern hospital.

"There is a little girl here who brings me flowers sometimes," he wrote Ruth. "She is a year or two younger than Clarissa and she has a doll with a cloth head because the china one got shot away when her house was under fire. Her name is Camilla Calhoun and she likes to have me tell her about Clarissa's doll Hitty. Today she brought me a jasmine flower and said 'Send it to the Yankee doll.' So here it is."

And it actually was in the letter, though nothing more than a flat, brownish crumple of leaves.

Clarissa didn't seem very much pleased at first.

"I don't want her sending Hitty flowers," she said.

"Hush," said her mother, "thee must love thy enemies. It was a kind thought and thee has not suffered as that poor child has in this terrible War."

As for Ruth, she would have liked nothing better than to pack me off then and there to that little Southern girl who had been kind to John Norton. I felt relieved that the mails were too uncertain for this, as I had no wish to find myself under fire.

## CHAPTER XII
# In Which I Go Into Camphor, Reach New York, and Become a Doll of Fashion

It must have been toward the end of the Civil War that I had my first taste of going into camphor. This was an experience I was to have many times later on. It is hard to describe the sensation exactly, but I think it must be rather like this new-fangled fashion which people call "taking ether," when they must have painful things done to themselves. At any rate, when Clarissa Pryce was to be sent away to a boarding-school for young Quaker girls, I was packed up with many white balls that gave out a strong smell. Gradually, this overpowered me, so that I had no idea of what went on about me or of the passing of time.

I know now that it must have been nearly two years that I lay in this state before the box was opened. Meantime, it had been removed from the Pryces' Philadelphia attic and sent to distant cousins in New York with some old furniture and odds and ends of material. But somehow or other, my box, which contained also a great many pieces of silk and ribbon, became separated from the rest by an absent-minded expressman who had a wagonful of goods to deliver. My box was, therefore, carried, along with a couple of trunks, to the attic of a house on Washington Square. Even after that it was some time before anyone bothered to open it. I was unearthed at last by Miss

Milly Pinch, who had come to stay a fortnight and sew for the Van Rensselaer family. She was rummaging about for some lace to edge Isabella Van Rensselaer's new petticoats, when she found me.

Instead of packing me up again or bringing me to one of the children, she carried me down to her own room, where she hid me on the top shelf of her wardrobe. I began to feel that I had not fared very well after all, but I changed my opinion that night after supper when Miss Pinch brought me out and began measuring me for new clothes. I can see her now as I write, her thin, plain face with its near-sighted blue eyes bent over me, her mouth bristling with rows of pins in a way that was terrifying to behold. Her fingers were thin and yellow, but she could do marvelous things with them, as I was soon to learn.

"I'm going to show them a thing or two," she said, for she had a way of talking to herself when no one was about. "When I've got you dressed up, Miss, they'll see that I'm as good a dressmaker as any of these fancy ones from Paris. I'm only fit to sew children's petticoats and second-best dresses, am I? Well, we'll see."

She snapped her lips together so tight at those words that I feared she would swallow some of the pins. After a while I learned not to agitate myself about this. Miss Pinch was gifted above most when it came to handling pins. As for her needle and thread, she was equally skillful, and I have never seen anyone who had such a way with scissors. She used enormous ones, too. At first, I felt sure those great shining blades were going to meet and snip me in two. But again I survived, to reappear in an outfit that would have been considered positively scandalous by the families of all my former owners.

You see, I was to be Miss Pinch's masterpiece, her proof that she was a fashionable dressmaker and not merely a seamstress by the day. She was far too poor to buy a model, so when I turned up it was like an answer to her prayers. She certainly spared no pains upon me. I used to wonder how she could keep awake to work on my things after she had been sewing all day. But I think she loved making tiny ruffles and pin tucks, setting in darts with such fine stitches it seemed no human hand could have made them, and fitting my things again and again to make sure every fold and gathering was right. All through those solitary evenings in the back bedroom, she kept up her queer fragments of talk, so that I came to have an odd and rather jumbled idea of the various members of the household.

"Humph," she would say with a sniff, "so Miss Lily must have mother-of-pearl buttons and three rows of braid to her basques, must she? And a taffeta for the next Assembly so she'll have plenty of partners. Well, I could tell them a thing or two and how unbleached muslin's too good for her when she's in one of her pets."

Or again, as her fingers whipped and stitched and shaped my tiny garments, I would hear her muttering threats such as:

"Just let Master Harry try hiding my thimble again and I'll go straight to his mother and tell her how the china shepherdess on the drawing-room mantel came to be broken." Then, with a particularly spirited snip of her scissors, "And Miss Isabella needn't think because of her big eyes and those curls that she's better'n the rest of the world. Telling me she won't wear the petticoats because they've only got Hamburg edging and two rows of tucks instead of three, the little peacock!"

And Miss Pinch's face would grow as sharp as her name and two round spots of red would come into her cheeks, till what with the pins bristling from her mouth and her long scissors besides, I would grow quite terrified of her.

But how she could sew! I am sure no doll ever underwent so great a change in two short weeks. No butterfly emerged more resplendent from its cocoon than I from the hands of Miss Milly Pinch. Except for my corals, only my chemise remained of my former wardrobe. I doubt if this would have been kept had she not thought it a remarkably fine piece of linen cloth. How is it possible for my poor pen to do justice to my new attire—to the watered-silk dress with draped skirt, fitted waist, and innumerable bows? How can I describe the blue velvet pelisse embroidered with garlands no bigger than pinheads? How tell of the little feathered hat and the muff of white eiderdown?

"There, now," said Miss Pinch, turning me round when my toilette was finally complete, "you're as stylish as anyone from here to Fourteenth Street, and I don't care if I do say so!"

So I became a doll of fashion, which only goes to show that we never know from what direction miracles will come. Who would have turned to shabby, hard-working Miss Pinch to be made over into a fashion-plate?

That next day I spent on her bureau, staring in fascinated wonder at my reflection in the mirror. I could not get over the queer effect of my familiar features in such new and wonderful attire and despite all the warnings I had heard from the families of both Little Thankful and Clarissa, I could not but find it extremely pleasant to be as well dressed as the pictures of the people in "Godey's Lady's Book," which lay open beside me.

Then suddenly, without any warning, the door opened, and instead of seeing Miss Pinch's face in it, there appeared the features of a very pretty little girl of eight or so. She had such pink cheeks and bright eyes and thick chestnut curls that I was enchanted. Her clothes, too, were handsomer than any other child's I had ever seen, for she wore a plaid silk with scallops of crimson braid and ever so many small gilt buttons. She peered all about the room cautiously, then, closing the door softly behind her, she came over to the bureau. The look of surprise on her face grew and grew as she examined me. When she had seen every smallest ruffle and pin tuck, she carried me away, down several flights of stairs and into a big hall with long gilt-framed mirrors.

A tall lady in a sealskin jacket and small hat with ostrich plumes was just coming in at the door. The little girl ran to her and held me out.

"Why, what have you got there, Isabella?" asked the lady, taking me from her hands. "Where in the world did you find such a thing?"

"In Miss Pinch's room," she answered, "and I mean to have her, for Miss Pinch is too old and ugly to play with dolls."

"How often must I tell you to keep out of the servants' rooms?" her mother reproved her.

"I saw her through the door," Isabella explained, which was the truth, in a way, but not all of it, as I well knew, "and see, she has a real fitted waist. It's made out of your old blue silk and the pelisse is from Lily's velvet."

"So they are," said her mother, examining them. "It doesn't seem possible that Miss Pinch could have made anything so stylish."

Unfortunately, at that very moment the dressmaker had come to the door to call Isabella up to a fitting. She heard the words and saw them bending over me.

"If you please, Mrs. Van Rensselaer," she said primly, "that's my property and I would thank you to keep Miss Isabella from meddling in what's none of her affairs."

I think Isabella's mother was annoyed that Miss Pinch should be in the right for once. She was tired from an afternoon of shopping and her tongue was sharper than she realized. She said afterward that she had not meant to hurt the seamstress's feelings. Well, a good many sharp words passed on both sides and Isabella interrupted every other minute to say that she meant to have me.

After some questioning, it came out where Miss Pinch had found me and that she had dressed me in the evenings.

"Then she does belong to us, Mamma!" cried Isabella. "She does if she came out of your attic and has clothes of your silk and Lily's."

But Miss Pinch was equally firm. She said she was sorry but I was her property and she meant to exhibit me as a model to show she was a better dressmaker than most people gave her credit for being. I listened to the whole scene and felt very uncomfortable, because they all said so many unpleasant things. I have no idea how it would have ended if Isabella's father had not come in and insisted on knowing what was the matter. He was a portly, polite gentleman with brown whiskers and a great many seals dangling from his watch chain. When he had heard both sides, he gave his verdict.

"The doll," he began, clearing his throat solemnly.

"Her name is Hitty, Father," prompted Isabella, who had already explored my underwear.

"The doll Hitty," he continued, "is undoubtedly Van Rensselaer property, since she came out of our attic, but her clothes are Miss Pinch's, since they would be nothing but scraps fit for the waste basket had it not been for her skill." He bowed to her very politely and she actually smiled in return.

"But, Father," put in Isabella, "what use is she without her clothes? And what use will her clothes be without her?"

"Exactly," he agreed. "I couldn't have put the case more simply myself. I believe, my love," he added, turning to his wife, "that Isabella has a legal turn of mind."

"Mind!" I heard Miss Pinch sniff under her breath. "She's got a temper, that's what she's got!"

By this time, however, Mrs. Van Rensselaer was sorry for what she had said, and Miss Pinch felt better because Mr. Van Rensselaer had been so polite to her. A little more discussion took place and at last it was agreed that I was to be bought for Isabella. Furthermore, her mother was to recommend Miss Pinch and her sewing to a modiste's establishment on Stuyvesant Square. I was to be taken over to prove what wonders she could perform with her needle. You can imagine how happy I was over the arrangement.

Although Miss Pinch was right about Isabella's temper and certain other shortcomings, still she was an attractive child—one of the most beautiful and high-spirited I have ever known. I must confess that I greatly enjoyed my stay with the Van Rensselaers of Washington Square, though I fear that my late Quaker owners would have deplored the worldliness of their ways.

Isabella had at least a dozen dolls in her nursery, but she preferred me to all of them. It began by her interest in my elaborate costume, but later I am sure that she came to care for me almost as much for myself. At any rate, she defended me against all criticism, and once I remember, when a caller remarked that I was "not exactly a beauty," she lost no time in replying: "Well, neither are you!"

I saw little of her older sister Lily, who attended a young ladies' seminary several streets away, besides being busy with lessons in music and dancing and the art of flower-painting. Isabella and her brother Harry, who was ten, and two years her senior, were taught at home by Harry's tutor, Mr. Jerald. Mr. Jerald was a pale, serious young man, who apparently loved Latin more than anything else in the world. He was much more interested in getting Harry far enough along to read a book he called "Caesar" than he was in putting Isabella through her fractions and spelling lessons. In short, Isabella did about as she pleased.

She was her father's pet, being the youngest and such a gay beauty. He often took her with him on long walks and read to her an hour each evening from "Nicholas Nickleby." I was usually present on these occasions. As had been the case with my other owners, my smallness appealed to her. She almost never left me at home, whether she was off for a shopping expedition with her mother to the merchants of Fourteenth Street, or to drive with her in the barouche when she paid calls on Stuyvesant Square or along Fifth Avenue, or when she went with Harry to learn the waltz and polka at Monsieur Pettoe's dancing school the other side of Washington Square.

Until then the only dancing I had seen was sailors' horn-

My spirit was willing enough but my pegs were not.

pipes and those performed by the savages, so Monsieur Pettoe's ballroom with its polished floor, the square piano and violin playing while all the feet wove in and out in the intricate steps of the lately imported dances from Paris, filled me with amazement. Isabella usually left me with Annie, her mother's maid, who brought us there each Friday, but once I remember she set me up on top of the piano. I have never forgotten how it felt to have the music going on directly under me. I seemed to be part of it and as I watched the children waltzing I determined that I, too, would acquire this graceful new accomplishment. But it was not so easy to do as to see, I discovered that night when I practiced in the privacy of the nursery after everyone was in bed. My spirit was willing enough but my pegs were not. It was the old difficulty of my legs' being each in one piece and not made to move separately. So though I could remember the music of the "Roses and Mignonette" waltz they had played that afternoon, and though I knew the steps my feet ought to take, still I was powerless to lift them in more than a clumsy thump or two.

So I put the idea of dancing from me. I am not one to give up easily, but I do know the impossible when I meet it.

That year I was to see another celebrated gentleman, one even more famous than Mr. Whittier. It came about entirely by chance on a walk which Isabella and her father were taking one Sunday morning. The weather was so snapping cold that Isabella's cheeks were almost as red as the new cashmere dress she wore under her blue pelisse. She had a red feather in her little round hat, too; I remember I thought it looked very nice against her bobbing curls. I was also in my best, eiderdown muff and all. Mr. Van Rensselaer had been to leave some calves'-foot jelly and a bottle of sherry with a sick friend. We were returning along the east side of Fifth Avenue when the event occurred.

Just as we neared the entrance to the Brevoort House, a hotel of fine proportions and pillars, several gentlemen were seen to come out. People were always coming and going there, so I thought nothing of this till I heard Isabella's father saying in a low voice, full of interest: "Why, I do believe that is Dickens in the greatcoat. I heard he was to stay at the Brevoort, but I had forgotten."

I fell at the feet of Mr. Dickens.

"Not Charles Dickens, Father?" asked Isabella with more awe in her voice than I had ever heard before. "Not the man who wrote 'Nicholas Nickleby'?"

"Certainly, my dear, I'm sure I cannot be mistaken, so take a good look at him."

Although Isabella was usually a most composed child, this seemed too much for her. Indeed, she was so overcome that she dropped me almost at the very feet of the great man. I felt overcome myself, humiliated to be in such a position before him. But Mr. Dickens rose to the situation, or rather stooped to it, for he bent and picked me up most gallantly. With a pleasant bow and smile he returned me to Isabella while the two men with him and Mr. Van Rensselaer looked on with amused expressions.

"Oh, Father," said Isabella, when the men had driven off in their carriage, "did you see? He picked up Hitty himself. And it was his right hand, too, the one he writes all the books with!"

"Yes," her father agreed, "it will be quite a story to tell your grandchildren."

But Isabella did not wait to tell her grandchildren about it. Everyone we met must hear the story and for months to come I was brought out and exhibited as the doll who had been held in the very important right hand of Mr. Dickens. I do not wish to seem proud, but I cannot help wondering how many other dolls can boast of such an honor?

## CHAPTER XIII
# In Which I Spend a Disastrous New Year's and Return to New England

I might still be in the Van Rensselaer family and being exhibited to Isabella's grandchildren, if it had not been for the New Year's celebration of the following year. In those days, it was a far more important holiday than Christmas, and for weeks New York kitchens in that neighborhood had been active with preparations. Wonderful cakes were baked and iced, cookies and ginger nuts made, and mysterious bottles were brought up from the cellar to be ready for the hot toddies, eggnogs, and punches that would be served from New Year's Eve and on through the next day. Lily Van Rensselaer was pronounced of an age to receive callers with her mother and father in the drawing-room, but Harry and Isabella were still considered too young to take much part in New Year's doings. They made up for this the days before by stealing down into the kitchen and nearly driving the cook and maids distracted with their samplings of everything. But when the day itself arrived and they were banished to the nursery upstairs, they felt very rebellious and aggrieved.

From eleven o'clock on, there had been continuous rings at the front door bell and poundings at the knocker. The sound of voices and laughter and clinking china floated up to us. The streets were thronged with people going about to pay New

Year's calls. It was for this reason Isabella had been charged not to poke her nose beyond the front door. It was not a day for little girls to be abroad, for a many of the gentlemen had been indulging in far too many toddies and eggnogs, and there were, besides, groups of rough men and ragamuffins from the poorer parts going about to get what they could from begging or taking. We could hear some of these gangs singing rowdy songs as they went by, some dressed in fantastic costumes they had collected from rag bags and ash barrels.

Isabella stood the nursery as long as she could. Harry was no help, being completely taken up with a new carpenter's chest that had been given him, and the maids all too busy to amuse her. The parlor was out of the question, since no amount of teasing had prevailed on her mother and father to let her in. She therefore hung over the banisters till she was dizzy with watching hats and canes being laid on hall furniture.

"I don't care if it is New Year's," I heard her say finally, "I'm going out myself. I guess I can make a call on Mr. Jenkins if I want to."

Mr. Jenkins was a friend of her father's, the same, in fact, to whom we had taken the sherry. He was a bachelor who lived in a big brownstone house and always made much of her. So presently Isabella had got herself into her outdoor things and with me in hand was slipping cautiously down the stairs. She waited behind the velvet portières of the drawing-room door, and when the hall was empty except for the tall silk hats and the canes, out she slipped. I knew it was very wrong of her, but I could not help a certain pleased excitement at the idea of being abroad by ourselves at such a time. Twilight was coming between the houses, but some faint sunset color still showed behind chimney pots and the trees of Washington Square. The sidewalks were thronged with hurrying people, and lights were beginning to stream out of windows on either side of the avenue. I think Isabella feared she might meet some friend of the family who would return her to the fold, so she decided to take a less familiar, roundabout way. Accordingly, we went west in the direction of Sixth Avenue.

Here all the shops were tightly shuttered, save for a chemist's or two, where great red or green jars threw out jets of colored light. Carriages and an occasional horse car rumbled by, but it was less crowded than on shopping days. Mr. Jenkins lived quite far uptown, in the "wilds of Twenty-third Street," Mr. Van Rensselaer used to say jokingly. Somehow, it seemed farther than usual that night, and I suspected that Isabella would not have minded turning back by the time we were nearing Sixteenth Street. But once she had made her mind up, nothing could change it, not even her own feelings. So on we went. The wind blew a gale round all the corners and a few flakes of snow were beginning to fall. Suddenly, out of nowhere, or so it seemed, a crowd of urchins in blackened faces, cast-off hats, and an odd collection of old clothes bore down upon us. They must have been waiting in an alley for just such a chance to have sport with a well-dressed child out by herself. They were an odd-looking lot of boys of assorted sizes, with sticks and old umbrellas, which they waved with war whoops. They wanted pennies and I have no doubt if Isabella had had any to give them they would have let us pass peacefully.

But Isabella had no pennies, and seeing that no one was

about to put a stop to their sport the boys set upon us fiercely.

"Tassels on her boots," screamed their leader, "get the tassels on her boots!"

What good they would be to those boys I could not make out, but go for them they did, though Isabella kicked out with all her might and used her fist. She had me in her other hand, which did not help matters.

"You'd better leave me alone," she cried, "or my father'll have you all put in jail."

"Ha, ha," mocked the leader, "my father'll have you put in the reservoir on Forty-second Street, and then you'll look a pretty sight. Oh, won't she, though, boys? Come on, let's take her there."

"Don't you dare to touch me," stormed Isabella, who was nearly in tears and at the same time stamping her foot with rage. "I can scratch and I can bite, too."

I could see from this that she had abandoned all hope of help from anyone but herself. Isabella was no coward. I hardly think many little girls would have stood up alone against that wild-looking troupe as she did. But of course she was no match for them, and in the end they had torn off her squirrel tippet and her ostrich feather, and one particularly unpleasant boy had snatched me rudely from her hand. The next thing I knew there was a whistle in the distance.

"Skip!" yelled the leader, and almost before the sound had died away the whole gang had scattered as by magic.

I had a glimpse of Isabella standing at the head of the alleyway, imperiously calling to a policeman and several passersby to come to her aid. Her hat with its red feather lay in at least six different bits, one sleeve was torn off at the shoulder, and the snow was falling on her disheveled hair and flushed face. I never saw anyone look quite so beautiful or so furious.

New Year's is anything but a name to give me pleasant associations. It would have brought tears to poor Miss Pinch's near-sighted eyes to see what those boys did to my fine outfit. They carried me away with Isabella's squirrel tippet for trophies. The tippet was taken by the leader, and since no one seemed particularly anxious for me, they decided I would make an excellent torch to set on fire.

Fortunately, they were then distracted by an invitation from some other boys to join a raid which was about to take place on a bakery shop. This turned into more of a fight than they had expected and presently there were more whistles and the word was passed round that the police had been sent for. Once more the gang scattered in different directions. One of the dirtiest boys stuffed me, headfirst, into his pocket with all my ruffles crushed and the lace of my underwear catching on buttons. Later, another boy thrust me roughly on the end of a stick and carried me like an effigy at the head of their procession. The point of the stick made a rent clear through to my chemise, and the snow, which was now falling steadily in big flakes, added to my bedraggled state. Up one street and down another they went—stealing ash cans and doorplates, throwing stones at unshuttered windows, raiding basement doors and unprotected passersby, and generally making a nuisance of themselves.

At last, the pangs of hunger sent them scattering to their various homes, if the crowded tenements and shanty cabins in vacant lots where they lived could be so called. I feared that I was going to be tossed into the gutter and trampled by the first horse's hoofs, when one of the gang asked if he might have me.

"For the kids at home," he volunteered, rather shame-facedly.

A hoot went up from the rest. But the boy who had been carrying me on the stick handed me over.

The next thing I knew I was the center of attention in a very different sort of room from the one I had left. An Irish cabdriver's family were eating their New Year supper in the kitchen of a tenement over a livery stable off Perry Street, and it was here that the boy, Tim Dooley, brought me. The table had no cloth, and the china was thick and cracked. It seemed to me that at least ten children of assorted sizes were gathered round it, all clamoring for the stew a big, red-faced woman was ladling from a kettle on the stove. As soon as the children caught sight of me, they turned their attention from the stew and all demanded me at once.

But Tim had plans of his own. A little cousin named Katie and her mother had come to spend New Year's with them and it was for her that he had saved me from the boys. I felt relieved that I was not to belong to any of the young Dooleys, for a more noisy and destructive lot of children I have never seen. Before the evening was over, I wondered that there was a stick of furniture left in the place or a single plate or cup on the shelves. Katie was not very strong or, I am happy to say, very boisterous. Tim had taken a great fancy to her, although she was only nine and he was going on fourteen. She was a pretty child with soft black hair and blue eyes and a rather sad expression like those in the engravings of good children in the little books of that time.

My clothes were in a deplorable state, but no one seemed

to think of doing anything about them, and when I saw the careless way the children went about in rents and rags, I could not feel very hopeful for the future. However, I was warm and safe and Katie lavished much affection upon me, so I could not feel it right to complain, though I could not but have pangs of regret at the loss of my finery.

But I told myself that it is no disgrace to come down a peg or two in the world.

At all events, I had a chance to go traveling by the new steam cars, an experience I might not have had if I had stayed on in the house on Washington Square. It was a long trip, from early morning till late at night, for Katie and her mother were returning to their home in Rhode Island. I felt terrified of the great black, snorting engines when I first saw them rushing along the station platform, but once we were inside the car and settled on the hard seats, I gave myself up to the pleasure of staring out of the windows. After the stagecoach days, this seemed nothing short of miraculous. To see fields and cows, towns and houses slipping away faster than sand from an hourglass filled me with amazement. Katie's mother seemed almost as impressed as I, for I heard her talking with a woman across the aisle about the advantages of traveling by steam.

"Yes," she said, wagging her head solemnly, "the inventions of men are terrible. I expect my Katie here'll live to see 'em take to the air."

"You're right," agreed her neighbor, "I'm thinkin' it's steam that makes the world go round nowadays."

We stayed that night with a family in Providence and the next morning drove over by wagon to Pawtucket. Here Katie and her mother, who was a widow, lived with a number of relatives—brothers, sisters, aunts, and cousins—who worked in a yarn mill. Katie's mother stayed at home and kept house while they were away all day. It was a small house for so many people, but they were off before the mill whistle blew at seven in the morning and returned in time for supper. Some of the uncles even worked on night shifts sometimes, so except for Sundays I saw little of them. Katie was too delicate to attend school or play much with the noisy boys and girls of the neighborhood. She was generally in the kitchen, watching the various pots and kettles her mother had on the stove, ready to call out when any threatened to boil over. Her mother could then be washing or ironing or tidying the rooms upstairs. I cannot say it was a very exciting life for me after what I had been used to; still, I knew I was a comfort to Katie, and that means much to a doll.

Heretofore I had spent little time in kitchens and now I grew familiar with the various jars and bowls and crocks on the shelves. I also took a new interest in spices such as ginger, cinnamon, and citron. They never failed to bring back to me memories of the Island and far places. Indeed, one day when Katie's mother gave her a nutmeg to grate I was quite overcome by the memory of the monkeys about my old temple, especially the monkey who had brought me one of these. Sometimes I sat on the shelf directly over the fire with steam rising in clouds about me from the old black teakettle, and once I narrowly escaped falling into the doughnut fat.

One warm spring day, Katie sat too long on the doorstep and took a bad cold. She was put to bed and dosed and done up in red flannel, but without much good's coming of it.

Finally, one of her aunts fetched a doctor in and he said she was a very sick child and must go as soon as possible to a place he knew in the country where they gave children proper food and care. Her mother cried and carried on over this, but the rest told her she mustn't be foolish, and so after a few weeks Katie was better and pronounced ready for the change. Her things were done up in several boxes and she and I were both put aboard another train in the care of a kindly conductor. It wasn't such a long ride this time and after a while we were set down at a country station where a man in a buggy met us.

This was the hired man, who worked on the farm that was to make Katie completely well by the end of the summer. It was July, I remember, and the fields on either side of the road were yellow and white with daisies and black-eyed susans. I had not seen these since the days in Maine, and it seemed next best to meeting the Prebles again. The hired man's name was Amos. He was very pleasant and talkative all the way. He pointed out different farms we passed and told how many cows and pigs and chickens they kept. But Katie was more interested in how many children there were in each family and he was never quite so sure about that.

Mrs. Brackett met us when we pulled up at the back door of a white farmhouse. She was fatter than anyone I had ever seen before, and when her apron was tied round her waist you couldn't see the string, it sank in so deep. She had three children of her own and took as many more in to board, so she knew how to get on with them and what to say when Katie was homesick in the night and cried for the kitchen and all her family of uncles, aunts, and cousins. Mrs. Brackett approved of me because she said I was "a nice practical size," and she thought I looked as if I would be considerate of other people. She seemed to think that was the most important thing to be. At least, she was always telling the children about it.

I did not see much of the other children my first weeks there, because I stayed in Katie's room most of the time. Then one afternoon she took me out with her to have a ride on a hay wagon. Amos had promised that all the children should go. The six children, Amos, and I all rode in the empty hayrick to the meadow, where the hay was piled. We sat under a tree and waited while Farmer Brackett and he pitched it in till the cart looked higher than the barn doors. Then one by one the children were swung up and settled in the hay. I had never before sat so high up. It was a grand sight to look out over the rolling meadows, to the woods and hills and farms that were like those I had known first of all. It was exciting, too, when the horses began to pull and we lurched and swayed along over the ruts, with the branches of elms and maples brushing our faces as we ducked under them. The children screamed and shouted and sang as we went. Katie sat a little apart, for she was still rather shy of them. She held me in her lap and looked off dreamily to the river and the distant Brackett farm. Suddenly Willy Brackett began to cry and jump about.

"Oh," he squealed, "there's mice under me. I'm sitting on a nest of mice!"

He didn't mind that, but the three girls did. They began to cry and crawl away so that it is a wonder none of them fell over the edge. At last Amos had to stop the horse and climb up to quiet them. He stuck his pitchfork in the hay and finally succeeded in finding the nest, which he put out in a nearby field, tiny pink mice and all. He was far too kind-hearted to let any harm come to them, and he told the little girls not to be afraid if they sat on any more. But in the excitement Katie let go of me. Somehow or other I was trodden down under the children's feet and became more and more deeply buried in the hay. It was not until we reached the barn, however, and the children had been lifted off that my loss was discovered.

"Never mind," I heard Amos tell Katie, "I'll find her for you when I pitch the hay into the loft."

I was torn between my hope that he would find me and my fear of the exceedingly sharp prongs of his pitchfork. But I think Amos must have forgotten what a small doll I was, for I was tossed up in a big bunch of hay without ever being noticed at all.

Later on, he brought the boys and Katie, too, and they all went on a search for me in the loft. I could hear them very near, sometimes. Their hands almost touched me several times but never quite.

"I declare that doll acts plumb witched away to me," I heard Amos declare, and I wished I could tell him that his great boot was at that moment all but on me.

More hay was pitched in next day, and I suppose in time the children gave up looking for me. We are easily forgotten once we are out of sight, I have discovered, and I have no doubt that as Katie grew stronger and could romp and play with the others she no longer felt the need of my company.

Well, it was far from unpleasant in the hayloft. A softer bed I could not have found or one more sweet and warm in winter. More than one season's mowing was tossed in over me, and gradually I became shifted about so that I lay in a far corner where the hay was practically never touched. I had plenty of

Sometimes they would wash my face too.

time for reflection during the years that followed. Barn swallows and field mice were my only company. I came to be upon the most friendly terms with them, especially the latter. I saw whole generations of field mice grow from babyhood to maturity. Indeed, during some of the coldest winter weather I was very glad to be near to them for warmth as well as for companionship. A hayloft is not the neatest place in the world, and as time went on I grew very dusty. Sometimes the mice took pity on my sad state and when they were washing off their babies' faces, they would wash mine, too.

## CHAPTER XIV
# In Which I End My Hay-Days and Begin a New Profession

It was not the amiable Amos, but a different hired man who finally pitched me out of my hiding-place and into a cow's stall. I think I should probably have met my own end and caused the cow considerable discomfort if a small boy had not noticed me in time to effect my rescue from her jaws. He carried me out of the barn and into the farm kitchen where a new farmer's wife was cooking breakfast for two young men who were boarders there. They were artists, and one painted hills and houses and cows under trees, scenes he called "landscapes," while the other did pictures of people he called "portraits." It was this one who took such an interest in me. He gave the boy who had found me a quarter for me. Then he set me up on the table between his friend and a dish of eggs and declared that he meant to adopt me for his mascot from that day on.

The farmer's wife and his friend didn't seem much impressed by me. Indeed, she said I was the homeliest creature she'd ever met "outside of a scarecrow." But the Artist, whose name was Mr. Farley, said she didn't know true character when she saw it. After that I felt better, and when he carried me in his canvas sack on a sketching expedition next day, I felt quite like myself again in spite of the way my dress had gone into tatters and my coral beads broken and scattered to the four corners of the hayloft. Mr. Farley was painting several portraits of people in the neighborhood, and when he took me out and showed me to one of the young ladies who was sitting to him, she agreed to fit me out in respectable clothes.

She was a rather harum-scarum young lady, much more given to riding a horse and dancing than to plying her needle. But she did rip off my old dress and petticoats and make me a new set of clean but plain things. She showed Mr. Farley my chemise with the cross-stitching. This had faded so they could hardly make the letters out. But at last they did and Mr. Farley said he felt better now he knew my name. He said I must keep it next my person always.

The only thing that can be said for my new dress was that it had a brown-and-white china button at the back of the belt. Being a man, Mr. Farley was not critical of my new outfit. However, he personally cleaned the dirt from my face with turpentine and one of his own paint rags. He declared he was going to do my portrait soon. Sure enough, his next order was to paint a little girl, and he allowed her to hold me while he amused her with imaginary accounts of how I came to be in the hayloft. I could not but think my real adventures far surpassed those he made up for me. However, the child was interested and kept still, which was all that mattered to Mr. Farley. Indeed, her portrait and mine were considered equally successful.

So began my career as an artist's model.

After that, whenever he did portraits of little girls, I was pressed into service, and as Mr. Farley was an artist who traveled all over the country painting his pictures, my likeness must still be preserved in many places. Figuring as I did in so many canvases, I came in time to be quite a famous character in a small way. Some of you, perhaps, have seen my features in some family portrait, and several times Mr. Farley did me in what he called "a still-life group." This did not appeal to me greatly, for I found it trying to be in such close quarters with dried grass in vases and onions. I much preferred the children.

One shock which I experienced during this time was a sight I caught of myself in a looking-glass. Heretofore my glimpses had been so fleeting that I had not realized what a change my years of experience on sea and land and in haylofts had made in my appearance. There was scarcely a vestige left of the bright pink cheeks the Old Peddler had given me. My eyes were a worn-out blue now and the grain of my ash wood was beginning to show through. No, my complexion would never be what it had been, and I was just feeling rather depressed about this, when I overheard the Artist explaining to some one how superior I was to china-headed dolls, because, as he put it, I had "no trying highlights." No words can here express my gratitude to him for this.

I was Mr. Farley's traveling companion for a good many years, but though we visited New York and Philadelphia a number of times I was never able to see or hear news of my former owners. Later on, we went farther south, going by boats with big paddle wheels that churned the brown Mississippi River water into whiteness in a way that seemed amazing to one who had known only square-rigged whaling vessels and clipper ships. There was, however, one distinct disadvantage in not belonging to a child. Mr. Farley kept me packed in a box with his best camel's-hair brushes and his most precious tubes of paint, and we came out only after he was ready to begin work at his easel. I therefore missed seeing much of the country through which we passed on our way to New Orleans, that city which always recalls to my mind so much of elegance and revelry.

It was about carnival time that we arrived and Mr. Farley had some difficulty in finding a place to stay. The city was given up to elaborate preparations for the festivities—the processions, banquets, and balls which take place just before the beginning of the Lenten season—to think of anything else. Finally, however, he found two old ladies who agreed to let one of their rooms out to him. They lived in an old house in the French quarter with a courtyard full of greenery and an iron balcony that hung over the narrow cobbled street. There were just the two, Miss Annette and Miss Hortense Larraby, and a Negro woman still older, who had been a slave in their family before the war.

Miss Hortense was the older and handsomer of the two. She had been a beauty, her sister told Mr. Farley, and, indeed, her eyes were still very big and black, though without the shininess that they must once have had. The sisters must both have been great belles in their day. A large portrait of them painted when Miss Hortense was twenty and Miss Annette eighteen hung in the drawing-room, and I never tired of studying it. I found it hard to believe that the two wrinkled old ladies in their shabby silks could ever have been so young and pretty—Miss Hortense in canary-yellow brocade with her dark hair looped over her ears and her fingers strumming a guitar, while Miss Annette, in blue and sleek brown curls, leaned against her sister toying with a red rose. Sometimes I think they, too, were surprised at the change in their appearance. I have seen Miss Hortense stand a long time before the picture with a queer expression on her lips, and once I caught Miss Annette peering with just the same look into the long mirror between the French windows. But I never heard them mention such thoughts, not even to one another. It was only because I, too, knew what it was to change that I could understand all that must be passing in their minds.

Easter came late that year, so the weather was quite warm for the Mardi Gras festivities. Mr. Farley went about to see the processions go up and down the streets, but the two ladies were too frail to be in the crowds. They sat on their balcony listening to the music and twittered to one another about this or that float like a pair of tiny, ancient birds. I could see and hear them from Mr. Farley's room, which also opened out on the balcony.

Sometimes he took me out there, where all the new sights and sounds excited me after my long days and nights of quiet. There were so many black people always going by—women with bright calico round their heads, others balancing baskets on theirs as lightly as if they had nothing in them, old men and young calling their wares in soft, deep voices. I could not understand many of these cries, for the words were often in French. Even Mr. Farley, who had been to Paris, found it hard sometimes to tell, the queer way they made things sound. As the days passed and the weather grew into summer heat, the ladies retired more than ever into their cool parlors. They scarcely ever went out even at night, for their old servant bought what food they needed.

Occasionally, some very old lady or gentleman would ring the bell below and be ushered up to drink coffee. This was always a great event and I would hear the two chattering about it for days afterward. Sometimes, too, they were kind enough to invite Mr. Farley in for a cup. He always accepted, and once he brought me along to show them. I shall never forget the kind way their hands explored me. Their fingers were still tapering but worn and yellow as ivory. When they were through, they complimented him upon having such a refined and charming old doll, but they both assured him that I deserved a more elegant costume.

I was overjoyed a few weeks later when he was especially requested to bring me to see a friend who was drinking coffee with them. This proved to be a little old gentleman with the whitest of whiskers and the neatest of patent-leather shoes. He had been a friend of their dear brother's, they said, and he had come to arrange with them about lending a beautiful embroidered dress of their mother's to a Cotton Exposition which was shortly to be held. It was to be a great event, indeed, almost more so than Mardi Gras. It had occurred to the two that I might be dressed in the style of their own young days, which they insisted was much more graceful than any styles before or since, and be used as a model. They pointed out that I had a most unusual expression and that it would take only small bits of material to fit me out. They would dress me themselves and their friend and the committee would see that I was well placed and later returned in good condition. I felt quite overcome by the honor they proposed doing me and I could hardly wait to hear whether or not Mr. Farley would agree. Fortunately, he did. Indeed, he said it was an excellent idea, since he must leave for a month or more to paint portraits on several plantations.

"I know that I could leave her in no better hands than yours," he told them with a bow. "Besides," he went on, "I cannot but feel it is high time she saw something of her own kind. She has put up with my bachelor ways long enough."

Miss Hortense and Miss Annette took me completely into the little world of their quiet upper rooms. I became as much part of their lives during those next weeks as the mahogany and rosewood furniture, the black-and-gilt clock under the glass dome that their father had brought from Paris years ago, and the graceful figure of a slender china man with curling lovelocks, flowered waistcoat, knee breeches, and languishing air, who never moved from the exact center of the mantelpiece. They always referred to him as Monsieur Romeo, and he was treated with the respect and consideration due to a valued member of the family. There was an opening between his curved forefinger and thumb, and every day he had a fresh flower put there, while once a week Miss Annette went all over him with a damp cloth. I can see her now standing on an old mahogany chair, a lavender apron tied round her tiny waist, her frail hands wiping away any speck of dust that might dare to mar his beauty. I am sure it never occurred to them that he was less real than they. He was, however, far too proud to notice my presence.

My costume was a serious matter to the sisters. It must be cotton, for that was the nature of the Exposition. They talked of it for several days. Then, one morning, they each awoke with the same idea.

"Sister," said Miss Annette, a little timidly, "I have been thinking of the wedding handkerchief."

"And I," agreed Miss Hortense, nodding her head till the light twinkled on the high comb which caught up her white hair, "it came to me in the night. Let us get it out and see if there would be enough."

They had the servant drag out an old leather trunk and presently they were lifting from it a satin dress of such richness and sheen that it made me think of the luster on their best porcelain cups. There were tiny pointed slippers with ankle ribbons, a lace veil that looked as if spiders had spun it in moonlight, a pair of delicate mitts, a white-and-silver-bound prayer book, and the handkerchief. These were the wedding things in which their grandmother and mother and two aunts had been married. The sisters took each article out as if it were alive, and when they came to the handkerchief they were more deeply affected than I had ever seen them. It seemed that this had been woven across the sea from some cotton grown on their great-great-grandfather's plantation. Their own great-grandmother herself had embroidered it as she had been taught in a French convent. After her marriage, it had always been carried by every bride in the family. No one would have felt a wedding was complete without it. But now there would be no more weddings, since Miss Hortense and Miss Annette were the only ones left. They could not help crying a little as they bent over it together.

"See," said Miss Hortense, "there is the dove in the garland of rose buds. Do you remember how we used to look for it when we were children? It seems a pity that neither of us will ever carry it now. Not that I mind so much for myself, but you would have made such a beautiful bride."

"Oh, Sister," sighed the other, "it does not matter about

me, but you waited so long for Julian Chappelle, and then to lose him when the Yankees took Vicksburg!"

"I am not the only one whose betrothed the Yankees took," Miss Hortense answered, and I saw the color burn red for a moment on her cheek bones. "Oh, it was cruel, cruel. No one knows that better than you and I."

I thought that some of the Yankees could say as much. I remembered the days in the Pryce household when Ruth received word that John Norton had been wounded. Little did I think then that I should be living among those they denounced so bitterly or that I should meet only kindness at their hands. It was all so strange, beyond the understanding of a doll.

I was roused from these sad reflections by hearing Miss Annette suggest that I be dressed as a bride.

"It seems the only appropriate thing," agreed Miss Hortense. "The whole Exposition is to prove that we grow the finest cotton, so I am sure Great-Grandmother could not disapprove."

Such measuring and planning and fitting as went on before scissors were put to the heirloom. The sisters pored over old fashion books and cut tiny paper patterns, so that I should do them credit and not a scrap of the precious piece be wasted. There were fulled petticoats to be made first from other muslin, and these must have hems and feather-stitching so microscopic that even Miss Milly Pinch would have been forced to marvel. After much consultation, they decided to leave me my chemise, because they quoted an old motto that said every bride should wear "something old, something new, something borrowed, and something blue." They washed and

I was dressed as a bride.

bleached it with their own hands, however, and wondered who put the cross-stitch letters on. They placed a French knot of blue on my inner waistband, and—as for something borrowed—Miss Hortense declared there was no need of going out of their way for this, since I myself was a borrowed contribution to the Exposition. So day after day they snipped and fitted and stitched in the dim parlors, with the cries from the street sounding very soft and faint behind their closed blinds.

They were like children, or a pair of birds, the afternoon the last stitch was set in place. For once, I felt far superior to the china man on the mantelpiece on whom they had scarcely bestowed a glance for days. They set me up on the white-and-silver prayer book on the center table and regarded me in silent admiration for a long time. At last Miss Annette drew a long breath and touched my lacy veil with one finger.

"Sister," she murmured with awe, "it does not seem possible we could have done it ourselves. I could almost believe that the blessed saints themselves had come down to guide our fingers."

"Who knows but they have?" said Miss Hortense. "It seems nothing short of a miracle that there should have been enough to edge both sleeves."

Their friend the old gentleman was as good as his word and I had a place of honor in the section of the Hall devoted to cotton products. I sat in the middle shelf of a glass cabinet, with exquisite examples of skilled needlework above and below me. I was complete, even to a miniature bouquet of white flowers in a lace-paper holder, and there was a card in front of the shelf that told how I had been dressed by the two sisters out of some of the finest cotton ever woven or worked. Sometimes the crowd about my cabinet was two and three deep, and I was only sorry that the glass prevented my hearing the admiring comments.

There was nothing, however, to prevent my seeing all that went on, and for the first days I sat there I was in a continual state of amazement at the changes which had taken place in people's clothes. Even after my rescue from the hayloft and in spite of all my travelings I had had little opportunity to see the latest styles. Now I was able to see all the elaborately draped skirts, the bustles and basques, the enormous sleeves and tight jackets, the small bonnets no bigger than flat bows which were then worn over the bangs and curls or tumbling "waterfalls" of the ladies' hair.

It made me quite sad to see little girls going about with their mothers and fathers. Their open admiration of me was a comfort, however, for I realized that though styles may change and skirts be full or scant as fashion demands, still a doll is a doll. I was therefore more pleased when children cried because they could not take me home, or when little girls stood with their noses pressed to the glass of my case, than when the Governor or other famous visitors paused to compliment me.

One day, after I had been on exhibition for a number of weeks, I noticed a very big, sunburned man buttoned into a blue coat with braid and brass buttons and a wiry, tanned girl of eight or nine clinging to his hand. She was not so carefully dressed as most of the children who came there. Her clothes had been good enough once, but buttons were off, her over-skirt rumpled, and her jacket spattered. Her bangs of dark, straight hair were so long they kept getting in her eyes, and she carried a dilapidated red silk parasol. There would have been something arresting about the quick, free way she walked and the set of her dark head, even if she had not displayed such an unusual interest in me. She kept returning again and again to my case, and I thought the man in the blue coat and braid would never be able to get her to leave when closing time came. Next morning, almost before the doors were open, she was back again, her dark eyes going over every detail of my dress and me. Even through the glass I felt a certain fearlessness and spirit in her every motion. She was like an unbroken colt or a wild bird. The man in the blue coat was at her beck and call most of the time. It was evident she was the sort of child to get what she wanted.

She wanted me, and that is the whole truth in a nutshell, as Mrs. Preble used to say.

Finally, it got so that the man would come in the morning and leave her at the entrance. In a couple of hours he would return for her and they would go off to eat dinner somewhere. Then, like as not, she would be back to hover round my case till closing time. So it went for several days, and I must say I felt quite set up by such attentions. Nothing escaped her sharp, black eyes. That is how she came to notice when the key had been left in my case for a few minutes.

It happened in this way: The man in charge of that room was showing a group of honored guests over the various exhibits. One of them evidently expressed a wish to see me at closer range, so the man obligingly opened the glass door and I was handed about amid expressions of wonder and praise. The caretaker put me back and turned the key in the lock, but just as he was about to take it out, his attention was attracted elsewhere and the whole party walked off into another room. Nearly all the other visitors followed in their wake—nearly, I said, but not all. There was one who stayed behind. The dark little girl had watched her chance and now came noiselessly over to my case. She looked quickly all about to make sure no eye was upon her, then turned the key with steady brown fingers. The door swung open, her hand darted in and seized me firmly about the waist. It all happened in less time than it takes to tell. Another second and the door was locked again while I felt myself being stuffed into the red silk umbrella.

I have often tried to imagine the scene that followed, when the caretaker discovered that I was not in my place as he had left me. I can picture how he must have blinked and stared at the empty shelf, at the key still firm in the lock, and not a soul about to explain the mystery. Meantime, I was well out of the Exposition Hall. The dark little girl saw to that. Apparently, she possessed the skill and cunning of a serpent, for she slipped by the doormen, the red parasol that held its guilty treasure balanced lightly in one hand. She was well out of the way of suspicion by the time my loss must have been discovered.

Evidently she knew where the man in the blue coat was to be found, for soon I heard her talking to him. At least I supposed it must be the same, for she addressed him as Pa and told him she was tired and wanted to go down to the *Morning-Glory.*

"All right, Sally," I heard him say, "soon's I finish figuring on next trip's cotton shipment."

It was very uncomfortable being in the red parasol. The ribs stuck into me and I knew the cramped quarters must be hurting my veil and flounces. Only once did Sally reach down and feel to make sure I was still there. I must say I began to have considerable respect for her powers. How many children at her age, thought I, could keep such a secret without giving any sign?

And so, in time, I was taken aboard the *Morning-Glory*, which proved to be a river steamboat that plied between New Orleans and the upper Mississippi bringing down bales of cotton and fetching back merchandise and other cargoes on the return trip. Much as I regretted my theft from the Cotton Exposition, I could not but experience a feeling of pleasure and anticipation at being once more upon a boat and in the fortunate capacity of doll to the Captain's daughter.

Naturally, it was impossible for me to show my face on deck or in the open. Indeed, Sally Loomis—which turned out to be her full name—dared not even keep me openly in her cabin. I was therefore secreted in a small satchel made of sweet-smelling grass. This she kept on a shelf where she could get me out easily and where I was able to hear, if I could not see, a good deal that went on. From the first moment when she removed me from the parasol, Sally treated me with a curious mixture of awe and affection. I never knew when she took me out of hiding which mood I should find her in. She was a creature of violent and changing emotions. Sometimes, as on that first day, she seemed to regard me as some strange being out of the moon. She would sit staring at me so fixedly it seemed her dark eyes must actually bore into my wood. Or again she would press me to her and lavish all manner of sudden, impulsive caresses upon me. This alarmed me a good deal till I grew accustomed to her queer ways. Thinking it over now calmly in the quiet of the Antique Shop, I realize that the poor child had been too little with other children to know how to play. From infancy she had practically run wild, for her mother was an invalid, living on a distant plantation, and too ill to care for Sally. She was allowed to make trips with her father on the *Morning-Glory* whenever she pleased, and she pleased to most of the time.

I soon grew used to the sound of the paddle wheel churning the water and the steady chugging of the engines. The Captain made frequent stops to deliver small cargoes along the way and there were shouts and singing and much conversation when we put in at different places. I think it was at Natchez, a fine city of wharves and white old houses and much pleasant greenery, that I heard Captain Loomis read a notice about me which had appeared in the newspaper. It was several days old by the time it reached him.

"Come here, Sally, and listen to this," I heard him say as they sat on deck near our cabin. "It's all about that doll you took such a shine to at the Cotton Show." And he began to read aloud from the paper:

## MYSTERIOUS DISAPPEARANCE OF DOLL AT COTTON EXPOSITION

**Officials at loss to explain theft of valuable exhibit from glass case—Dressed by Larraby sisters in family heirloom—Police at work on all clues—Reward offered.**

"Well, now what do you think of that?" And he chuckled under his beard.

But Sally made no answer. I thought I detected something strange in her silence.

"Let's see," her father went on, without noticing this,

"disappeared yesterday afternoon, and this paper's three days old. Why, that was the very day you were there. She wasn't gone then, was she?"

"No, I saw her," Sally managed to reply.

In a sense it was the truth, but I could not help wondering what her father would say if he knew that I reposed in her grass basket within earshot of him that very moment.

"Seems it was only loaned to the Exposition," he went on as he read, "and they're real worked up over it. The man in charge of the room says he left for just a minute. When he got back the key was in the lock same's he'd left it, only the doll was gone from the case and not a soul in sight. He gave the alarm and they started searching everyone in the place, but there wasn't so much as a sign of it. They think maybe one of the caretakers took it and is too scared now to let on."

There was another long silence before I heard Sally's voice again.

"Pa," she said, "what would they do to anybody who took the doll? I mean, if they found out who did?"

"Do?" said the Captain, who had evidently begun to read of other matters, "oh, I expect what they always do to thieves—lock 'em up in jail. Well, it's lucky we went there when we did so's you could see the doll."

Sally lifted up her voice and began to sing with great gusto:

*Not for Joe, oh, no, no,*
*Not for Joseph, if he knows it. . . .*

a song she had lately learned. Later, when she slipped back to her cabin, she did not sing. She got me out very cautiously and sat staring at me with a queer expression. I could just make out her face in the moonlight.

"I don't care what that old newspaper says," she whispered in sudden defiance. "I shan't give you back, and they won't catch me, either."

She gave me one of her swift embraces and put me back in the basket. A little while later, I heard her singing more songs at the top of her lungs on the upper deck. Indeed, she made so much noise that her father shouted to her to "shut up" and go to bed or he'd see she sang a mighty different tune.

Nothing more was said about me. If the Captain came across further newspaper notices, he did not bother to read them out loud. Besides, the days were busier now, for we stopped less often and were heading upstream. At rare intervals, when Sally had me out of my basket, I caught tantalizing glimpses through the cabin window of wide stretches of muddy brown water, of fields of cotton or sugar cane where black people were at work, of flat green bayous and moss-hung trees, of old white-pillared houses behind tall trees and gardens. I longed to see more of this river panorama so new to me.

Well, one Sunday I had my wish gratified. Captain Loomis brought the *Morning-Glory* up to a rickety old wharf and went ashore to visit a friend who lived in a big plantation house a couple of miles back. He said Sally could not go, because he had too much to talk over to be bothered with her. She could stay on the boat, or, if she pleased, go ashore and see what was going on in a little cluster of cabins near the river. Some of the crew went on an expedition of their own, others slept or lolled on deck all day. No one paid any attention to her. So, emboldened by this, she brought the grass basket ashore with me in it. Once she was out of sight of the boat she took me out and carried me about as openly as if she had come by me in a proper way.

It was early afternoon, the sun shone blazing hot on the cabins and the little frame church toward which people were hurrying. They were all very black and beaming and they carried big palm-leaf fans and bunches of flowers, and some had tiny brown babies in arms. Sally and I followed after and took our places with other children on a board placed across two molasses kegs. It was even hotter in the church than outside. People were packed close to each other. The babies whimpered. Flies, bees, and bugs droned and buzzed everywhere in spite of the waving fans. The Man in the pulpit grew shinier and shinier as he talked. He used very long words and flung his arms about a good deal. I can remember only a little of what he said, but there was one part that made a great impression on Sally.

"My sisters an' brethren," he began, leaning far out over the box of a pulpit, "I is gwine to tell you one thing sure an' dat is if yo breaks de eight' commandment dat says: 'Thou shalt not steal,' you is gwine to be berry sorry. Some ob you, my brethren, has done broke it already. Some ob you has gone to jail an' suffered considrubble, but I tell you it ain't nothin' to the sufferin' you is gwine to get some day if you continues in sin and commandment-breakin'! An' don't you imagine, my brethren, dat you can go on foolin' de Lord forebber, 'cause He's got his eye right on you an dere ain't de smallest chile here dat He ain't able to look right down into his heart an' see if dere's sin hid down dere."

I could feel Sally stiffen at his words and she sat with her eyes fixed on his face more intently than I had ever seen them.

I knew what she was thinking, and though presently several children went to sleep at the other end of the hard bench and tumbled over with loud cries, she did not join in the general commotion that followed. Later, when the whole congregation had become worked up and all were singing and praying and crying out that they wanted to repent of their sins, she still sat quiet in her place. It was only after they all trooped out behind the preacher to follow him down to the river that she rose and went slowly after them. I have never seen a child more spellbound than she.

It was very exciting to watch the "baptizing" which now took place at the edge of the river. The Preacher got so excited he waded right in up to his middle. He began to urge everyone who wanted to have his sins washed away to come out to him. I couldn't help thinking that they might have chosen cleaner water for this. However, everyone was too worked up to bother about the thick brown mud. So in they began to go, girls in white dresses, tall brown youths with gleaming teeth and eyeballs, and even little children smaller than Sally. Mothers would thrust their babies into other women's arms and go rushing in to be ducked up and down by the Preacher, who went into a perfect frenzy with each new arrival.

"Glory, glory, glory!" he kept shouting as he sent each bedraggled convert to the shore, "anodder soul is saved. Whiter now dan de dribben snow."

I did not pretend to know anything about souls, but judging by the looks of their clothes when they waded back I could not feel he was very observant.

Everyone had been too busy being baptized, or watching others, to notice how dark the sky had grown or what immense thundercaps were rolling up. The sudden rumble of thunder came, therefore, without warning and sent the whole congregation scuttling to shelter. From their cries and looks of panic I guessed that they somehow connected this with the warnings of their Preacher. He got out of the river very quickly, I can tell you, and joined the scramble toward the huts. But as he ran he continued to call out words of admonition to his flock. The last I heard he was telling them that the thunder was a warning to those who had not repented to do so mighty quick.

Sally began to run, too, but in the opposite direction, toward the landing where the *Morning-Glory* was made fast. It was farther than it had seemed earlier in the afternoon. The sky was a queer greenish color now and jagged forks of lightning began to rip through it. The cottonwood trees swayed in the wind and the white patches on the bark looked ghostly in the strange light. I could feel Sally shiver and her breath come short as she sped on. We were still a good quarter of a mile from the landing when the storm caught us. Never have I seen anything quite like it for loudness of thunder, or brighter flashes of lightning or more heavy peltings of rain.

Crash! A tree went down a few yards ahead of us with a horrid ripping sound such as I had not heard since the topmast had shattered on the *Diana-Kate*. Sally crouched under another cottonwood tree and waited for the next flash of lightning to strike us down. She was crying and praying by turns now—a queer jumbled rendering of the Negro Preacher's words, mixed with her own fears and petitions.

"O God," she wailed, "don't let the lightning strike me dead and all of a heap, don't, please. I know I broke that commandment same's he said when I took Hitty out of the Exposition. I know I'm a sinner and there wasn't time for me to repent and get baptized, but just wait a little and I will. Please don't let the lightning get me this time." In spite of her pleas, there came the loudest rumble and crackle yet. She cowered against the tree trunk. I was back in the sweet-grass basket by this time, but I could hear every word she said, and the lightning flashes were not hid from me. "O God," she went on still more wildly, "didn't you hear me say I'm sorry I did it? Didn't you?" There was another peal very much nearer. "If you've got to strike somebody dead," she urged plaintively, "couldn't you take some of those little children over there that's all washed clean of their sins and haven't had a chance to do any more? Couldn't you?" Still louder thunder. "I tell you, I'll give Hitty back. I won't keep her another minute, Lord— look, here she is. You can have her, only just let me get back to Pa and the *Morning-Glory*!"

She was sobbing hysterically now. I could hear her even above the storm. Now she was running pell-mell down the bank toward the river. I knew only too well what she meant to do with me.

## CHAPTER XV

# In Which I Learn Much of Plantations, Post Offices, and Pin Cushions

Moses was not the only one to float about in a wicker basket on a river. But if I remember the story rightly from my days with Little Thankful's family in India, his sister kept a very careful watch over him. I had no such attention, and I doubt if the waters of the River Nile could possibly have been so muddy as those of the Mississippi. Although Sally's basket afforded me some slight protection, it nevertheless let in water aplenty. All my Exposition finery was soaked in no time and I bobbed about in my grass cage full of brown water. It must have been a good many hours that I could feel the rain pounding down, and the thunder continued to rumble overhead. I wondered if Sally Loomis had reached the boat safely and if she would regret her rash act of casting me in the river. I wondered, too, if she would confess her theft the next time she went to church. I told myself that with her queer, sudden ways she was like as not singing some new song she had learned from the crew and that I had disappeared clean out of her thoughts. Well, wondering is as near as I shall ever come to knowing.

In time, I came to rest. It was not, however, among bulrushes but between the wooden piles of an old landing, and I was fished up not by a Princess of Egypt but by a couple of

Negro boys out fishing in a flat-bottomed boat. They were going to use the basket for bait, so they did not feel particular enthusiasm at discovering me inside. Still, they chuckled a good deal over their find, and the smaller one, a boy who went by the name of Cooky, finally decided they might as well take me back to his little sister Car'line. They had no intention, however, of letting me interfere with their fishing, for they pulled away into a smaller but equally brown stream between flat green banks. I lay on my back in the bottom of the flat boat between a tangle of fishline, a net, a tin can of bait, and altogether too many flopping, slimy fish in various stages of expiring. Soon a couple of unfortunate frogs had been added and an exceedingly active turtle. He snapped his jaws in a terrifying way, so I tried to see nothing but the blue sky and dazzling sun ball above me.

"At least," I thought, "it is better than being tossed about at the mercy of every river current. I am drying off by degrees, and if I do the turtle no harm, he will doubtless not bite me." I could feel my bedraggled skirts stiffening and the mud caking on my face. "And mud is said to be good for the complexion," I added by way of cheering myself.

Toward sundown, Cooky and his friend hauled the boat well above some mud flats and took their catch home. They each lived with numerous brothers and sisters in the cabins belonging to a big white-pillared house which stood higher up behind some ancient, moss-draped live oaks. The fields where the men and women worked were on another part of the plantation, but the cotton had already been picked and sent away. It was going on late September and an off time in that part of the world. Crops were in and the workers had just received their wages. So everyone was in a happy frame of mind, from the oldest, wrinkled grandpappy smoking his pipe on the cabin doorstep to the fattest baby rolling on the dirt floor.

Car'line greatly resembled the picture of Topsy in the Pryces' copy of "Uncle Tom's Cabin." But I was hers from the moment her rolling eyes fell upon me in Cooky's hand.

"Dat ma chile," she said, as proudly as if I had been in the richest of silks instead of my brown, water-soaked dress that gave scarcely a sign of what it had once been.

"How you come by dat doll?" questioned Cooky's mother, as she stood stirring corn-meal mush over her fire. "You ain't steal it from the folks in de big house?"

When he had told her about finding me, she gave a shrill chuckle.

"Hey-lor'," she laughed, "jes' hear dat now. Fine 'most any kind ob contraption in Ole Ribber if you keeps on lookin'."

If the cabin was rather too small for all the children and grown-ups who must sleep in it every night, at least I did not lack for sociability. I was always near at hand when Car'line played with the other children, their shoeless feet stirring up great clouds of dust as they ran and scuffled. I liked to hear them sing, for their voices were softer and sweeter than those of any children I had ever met before. At night, too, there was always music in the cabins. Long after Car'line had dropped off to sleep in a heap of other children by the doorstep, I would listen to the men strumming their guitars or making the banjo strings twang and tinkle in a strange and delightful manner.

The first night I heard this, I remember I could not help thinking of the Island and the beating of the savages' skin drums. Not that it was the same tune, of course, only this music had the same stirring quality. It made me want to get up and dance as some of the girls and boys were already doing—but not the precise steps of the waltz or polka as taught by Monsieur Pettoe off Washington Square. No, this was a very different sort of music, indeed.

Sometimes they sang, too, strange and often sad songs that I never tired of hearing. These were occasionally about biblical characters. I recognized Moses, Jonah and the Whale, Noah, and King David. It seemed like finding old friends to hear about them again in such different surroundings. There were other songs I liked to hear. There was "Swing Low, Sweet Chariot," and "Oh, My Lord, What a Mornin'," and one that always made me feel queer twinges in my pegs that began: "My Mother Done Ride Those Big White Horses." I can hear those strings twanging and humming under their fingers now, even though it is a good many years ago and the smallest babies must all be grown up with children of their own by this time.

Winter was not the formidable affair it had been in my more northerly homes. With the coming of December there began to be preparations for the party which was always held at the big plantation house. To this everyone, down to the smallest child, was bidden. I began to hope that Car'line would not leave me behind in the cabin. Sure enough, when Christmas Eve came round and all the younger children were scrubbed and fitted out for the next day, Car'line begged a piece of plaid calico to make a dress for me. It was nothing more than a square of cloth with holes cut for my arms and a pin that stuck into me to hold it in the back. Still, I was so glad to have anything to cover the wreck of my bridal finery that I felt only gratitude. Car'line herself was resplendent in turkey red, her hair in eleven tight little braids each tied with a scrap of the same material. She was very good about the combing and braiding, though her sister Hatty who did this for her was severe.

"Stan' still now," she would command, as she jerked and pulled till the smaller child's eyes popped and her eyebrows turned up with the tightness of the braiding, "how you reckon you gwine be 'lowed past de big doors if you ain't no better dan foh ornery days?"

There was, however, no question of the door's being shut in anyone's face, for the Colonel and his daughters were generosity itself. Long tables were laid in the kitchens where chickens, hams, pies, and puddings melted away before the earnest munchings of the guests. Never have I seen such food or such appetites.

Car'line kept me in her lap during the meal and close to her turkey-red chest when we were admitted to the hall and enormous parlors. No wonder all the eyes rolled and the teeth gleamed white at the sight. The place was like fairyland, with the windows and stairways twined in green and hundreds of candles doubling themselves in gilt mirrors. The floors had been cleared, but at the far end of the longest room was a huge table heaped with gifts. Behind this stood the Colonel, an old man with white hair and mustaches, and his two daughters. One of these was plump and dressy. She had two little boys in velvet suits and curls who helped distribute the presents, while the other was slim and more quiet. She was unmarried and took care of her father. I learned later that she was the "Miss Hope" I had heard of so often down in the cabins.

All the children surged round the table like a hive of eager buzzing bees. Car'line kept being swept aside just as she came in sight of the presents—toys and candy for the younger ones and articles of dress or tools for the older guests. It seemed as if she would never get her present and I began to feel worried as I saw the supply dwindling. But Miss Hope came to our aid. She called Car'line over to her side. Car'line was so overcome by this attention that she could not speak at all and only stood grinning up at Miss Hope and holding me close. I suppose I must have showed very well against Car'line's turkey-red dress, or perhaps it was that Miss Hope had sharper eyes than most. Something told me that this was one of those moments which change the whole course of our lives.

"Why this is very strange!" I heard her exclaim, as she took me in her hands, very white, thin hands on which were several beautiful rings with green and red stones.

She hurried over to show me to her sister.

"Laura," she said, "you remember that little wooden doll we saw at the Exposition?"

"Why, yes," her sister answered without looking up from the gifts she was distributing, "what about it?"

"It was lost, you know," Miss Hope went on. "I read about it in the papers after we came back from New Orleans. I believe this is it. I don't see how I could be mistaken in the expression and the size."

They both took me over to a lamp and examined my features carefully. Then they removed the calico and discovered my spoiled finery underneath. After that there was no doubt. They called Car'line over and asked her all about me. She was too shy to answer, but when Cooky was summoned, he explained how he had fished me up in the basket months before. They also referred to Moses and the bulrushes, so I began to feel very important, indeed.

"We must return her at once," declared Miss Hope. "The paper said she was only loaned and there was a great to-do over her disappearance, if I remember right."

Car'line, who had been growing more and more doleful with all she heard, now burst into loud wails and buried her head against her mother's skirts. Her eleven pigtails quivered as she sobbed.

Miss Hope was distressed, the more so because it turned out that all the dolls on the table had been given out to other children. But at last she took me in one hand and leading the weeping Car'line by the other conducted us up to her bedroom. It was an immense room that looked even larger because of the dim light. Only two candles burned on either side of the mirror of her dressing-table. Her silver and ivory toilette things shone in the light. There were roses on a table by her enormous canopied bed and more roses on the chair covers and curtains. In one corner stood a cabinet with glass doors behind which I could just make out the forms of china figures and what appeared to be toys. Miss Hope put me on her bureau and then went straight over to the corner. She opened the cabinet and took something out. Then she came back to Car'line.

"I am sorry about the doll," she said very gently. "You see she doesn't belong to either of us, so we mustn't keep her. But I am going to give you the one I used to play with when I was a little girl. Her name is Mignonette and she came from France. My dear mamma made all her clothes."

Car'line was too surprised to do anything but stare. Miss Hope had to put the doll into her hands. I could see it was a very handsome one of kid and china with real hair and a ruffled white dress and pink sash. Car'line was beaming broadly as she carried it downstairs to show the others, but I heard Miss Hope give a little sigh as she stayed behind to lock the cabinet.

I must say it was pleasant being in Miss Hope's bedroom even for the week or so it took to have my clothes washed and a letter written about me to New Orleans. Miss Hope personally removed my things and washed them with her own hands. She marveled over the perfection of the wedding handkerchief and almost wept that the damage to it was irreparable. The brown stains would not all come out and there were rents too jagged for even her skillful needle to darn. My petticoats, being of newer goods, were less hurt, and my chemise came out almost as good as ever. I began to think that it must have been made of stuff as durable as my mountain-ash wood, though the cross-stitch letters had now faded to the palest of pink.

"I am getting so attached to the little old doll," Miss Hope told her father a few days later, "that I really hate to let her go. I don't know when I ever saw a more appealing face."

"Yes," he agreed peering at me out of his deep-set blue eyes, "a lady of quality, and character, too. One doesn't meet so many of her kind nowadays."

I have treasured his words for years. A compliment from such a gentleman is not received every day of one's life.

But Miss Hope was true to her convictions, so one day she wrote a letter to a friend in New Orleans, explaining how she had come by me and that I answered perfectly the description of the lost Exposition Doll. She put me in cotton wool in a small wooden box with what remained of my clothes upon me. Then she shut down the lid, sealed me in with wax, and sent me off to the same friend.

I cannot say how long it was before the box was opened. All I know is that when the lid was removed, several people were discussing my fate. These were two men and a lady, none of whom I had ever seen before. They examined me, but with the curt, cold manners of those not interested in dolls. It seemed Miss Hope's letter had come before I had. The men had been connected with the Cotton Exposition, but now it had been over for months and they did not know what to do with me. They had been to the two old ladies, only to find that one of them was ill and the other had no idea where the Artist might be. So I lay in my box in the drawer of a desk for a good while. Sometimes a hand would fumble about after pens or paper and I would be brought up to the light for a minute or two. Perhaps at these times there would be a remark made about someone's sending me somewhere, but then I would only be thrust in again.

At last, however, someone brought the Artist's address.

"It's where he used to live in New York," I heard them say, "so the doll will doubtless reach him in time."

Once more the lid was fastened down and I was sent off through the mail. I did not care for this method of traveling at all. It seemed a decided comedown to me after my previous journeyings by land and sea and river steamer. The cotton made a comfortable bed, however, and after the years I had spent in the close quarters of the horsehair sofa, I felt I had no right to complain.

Sometimes, too, if the top of the box were in a certain position I could hear, through a crack in the wood, what was going on. It was in this way that I learned how difficult it was proving to find Mr. Farley's whereabouts. The postman must have taken me to several different addresses, for I heard him inquiring whether any person by that name lived there. Always it was the same answer: no one had ever heard of him. I began to feel very uneasy over my future.

"Well," I heard a man's voice saying, "this goes to the dead-letter office."

You can imagine my feelings at those words. I felt my days were as good as numbered and every shaking or jarring of my box must mean I was to be taken out and burned or chopped up. It was a black time for me, and though I tried to reassure myself that my mountain-ash wood frame would yet come to my aid, I must confess that my usual good spirits deserted me. I quite longed for camphor to put me into a state of complete oblivion.

Well, there is no state which does not change some time or other, and at last the day came when I felt my box lifted down and shaken rather violently.

"Here," I heard a man say, "this goes with that lot of parcels. Done up in wood and don't weigh much. Maybe you'll be lucky enough to draw a pearl necklace, Charlie."

Of course I had no idea what was happening at the time, though I have since learned that every once in so often, when all the shelves of the dead-letter office become filled with unclaimed parcels, people are allowed to buy these for themselves. No one knows what is inside, so it is like grab-bag at a fair. There is much rivalry among the men and often a poor postman has been lucky enough to find a real prize.

The one who drew my box was disappointed when I did not turn out to be a valuable piece of jewelry. I was passed around amidst considerable mirth.

"Anybody want to swap with me?" my purchaser asked.

"All right," another said. "I'll give you this painted soap dish for her, though it's worth more."

I felt too humiliated to listen further.

But things moved very swiftly for me after that.

My purchaser carried me off with his other parcels. These were in a bag which was so full he carried me by hand. On the way home, he stopped to buy some tobacco at a little shop on a side street. Here he put his things down while he filled and lighted his pipe. When he left he picked up the bag and walked off, entirely forgetting about me. Soon I felt some one open my box and a fat woman was bending over it.

"Look at that, now," she said. "He forgot that box. I expect it was for his child, for it's got a doll in it. Well," she added putting back my cover, "I'll set it on this shelf. He'll be in again to ask for it likely."

Whether or not he ever did come back, I shall never know, for the very next day my box was caught up with several others.

"I believe this is her best grade of clay pipes," I heard some one say to a customer.

Evidently, he looked in only one box and supposed there were more in mine. At any rate, some one was careless enough to wrap me with two others and hand me over to a purchaser. I only vaguely realized what had happened, for of course I heard only scraps of talk and could see nothing while the cover was down. But when it was removed again I heard a very cross man scolding to someone about the mistake.

"I declare," he fumed, "if that stupid boy at the shop hasn't made a mistake. It's a nice thing to open a box that ought to be full of pipes and find nothing but an ugly old doll in it!"

I felt he could have found a good many worse things inside. I had been used to such kindness and admiration in the past that I grew quite depressed, especially when he threw me down with such exasperation that I bounded off the table to the hard floor. I was pretty well shaken in my pegs, I can tell you, but this was as nothing to the jolt my pride had received.

However, after the man had tramped out of the room, his wife picked me up, dusted me off with her apron, and set me on the window sill while she got dinner. I gathered myself together enough to look about me and discover that this was the kitchen of a flat overlooking a railroad station. Trains went to and fro under the windows all day and all night. The steam from the puffing, snorting engines rolled up in gray curls, laying carpets of coal dust and cinders on everything in sight. Indeed, it had so blackened the letters of the station sign that it was all one could do to make out the name, "Liberty Junction." The man, it soon developed, was ticket agent in the station and his wife ran a small lunch counter at one end of it. She baked pies and cookies and made doughnuts at home and carried them and a big pot of coffee over to the station every day. There were long spells between trains when she could go back to her kitchen or when she could sit and read any papers and magazines left in the waiting-room. She usually preferred to do this, which was how she came by such a variety of information.

"Jim," she told her husband a night or two after he had

found me in the box, "if you don't want that wooden doll, I'd like to try an experiment with her."

It sounded rather frightening, but still I preferred her handling of me to anything the man might do. He grunted an assent and soon she was thumbing an old needlework page in a fashion book.

"Yes," she said, getting out a measuring tape and taking my measurements, "I believe you'll do, even if you are kind of the worse for wear and I wanted one with a china head like the pattern."

I had no idea what her intentions might be, so for several days I watched her preparations with misgivings. I was in her workbasket now, along with innumerable spools of thread, papers of needles, darning eggs, unmended socks, and the usual conglomeration of scissors, emery, beeswax, thimbles, and tape. She took her work over to the station and I finally heard her telling a neighbor about her plan. I was to become a pincushion.

"Doll pincushions are all the thing," I heard her say, "like this in the picture. You stuff all round their legs and just leave out the arms and head. I wish I could afford a new doll, but I may as well experiment on an old one first. If it turns out any way at all, I'll give it to the fancy table at the church Fair next month."

So I was to be a pincushion! I cannot say the idea appealed to me. However, there was nothing for me to do but submit when she ripped off my clothes and dressed me in emerald-green silk. Once again my chemise was spared me, because it would help stuff me out before she began winding the layers of cotton batting from my waist down. Up to that time, I had found a good deal of fault with my legs and feet. I thought the Old Peddler had not given me so much agility of movement as he might, but now that I felt them being hidden from me in cotton wool, perhaps forever, I regretted all that I had ever said against them. But once more I was powerless to prevent their being sewed firmly in.

I cannot truthfully say that this was uncomfortable. But it was strange to become suddenly separated from the lower limbs which had been an active part of me for so many years. I could not grow used to seeing myself swell out like a balloon where I had tapered so decently heretofore. And I must confess that I could never get over an inward fear when people plunged pins into my padding. I reminded myself of Miss Pinch's mouth with the pins bristling in every direction, so altogether I was not very cheerful the day of the church Fair.

## CHAPTER XVI
# In Which I Return to Familiar Scenes

My spirits rose a little when the ladies at the fancy table were so openly admiring. The Fair was being held to raise money for the missionary fund, and when I heard that, I could not help remembering my Island days. I thought how scandalized the good ladies would be if they knew that the doll who sat among their other cushions, pin trays, and needle cases had once been the object of heathen worship.

Several people looked me over and were almost on the point of taking me, but for various reasons chose some other article instead. Finally, a lady named Maggie Arnold came along. Her eyes lighted on me almost at once.

"There," she said, "the very thing for Great-Aunt Louella's birthday. I've been racking my brain to get her something. She'll be seventy-five and she's got everything money can buy in this world, but I'd like to get her something kind of fancy."

So I was sold and wrapped in tissue paper.

Eventually, I reached Great-Aunt Louella, who lived in an old house in Boston. But I cannot say I was received with enthusiasm. The old lady was sitting at the breakfast table in black silk and spectacles, reading her birthday messages and unwrapping her gifts. She undid my papers, read the card, and peered at me critically.

"Humph," said she, putting me down, "I'd like to know

what Maggie Arnold thinks I'll do with a thing like that. Why, I've got enough pincushions in this house to stock an orphan asylum, let alone one that's trying to look like something else."

"Why, Miss Louella, that sounds real ungrateful, and on your birthday, too," reproved her old servant, who was clearing the table.

"I suppose it is, Mary," said the old lady, and she carried me in with her cards and other presents.

That afternoon she received several birthday visitors. I sat on the table and watched and listened to all that went on. It seemed good to be out of a box after so long, and I liked the big room with the coal fire burning in the little grate, the old portraits in their gold frames looking down on the heavy, carved furniture, and shelves full of books. One of the visitors was an old lady in a sealskin cloak and bonnet. She was smaller and more gentle than her friend and she made me think a little of the Miss Larrabys. The two friends sat and drank tea and chatted before the fire. They had been school girls together and called each other Lou and Pam.

"What's that you've got over there on the table?" Miss Pam asked suddenly, putting down her teacup.

"That," said Miss Louella scornfully, picking me up and setting me down on her friend's lap, "is the sort of contraption my great-niece Maggie Arnold sends me for a birthday present. I suppose I ought to be grateful she remembers the day instead of saying such things, but I declare I don't know what to do with it."

The other old lady was studying me with quite an interested air, feeling the wool stuffing to see whether or not I ended at the waist. She put on her glasses and held me close to her eyes, turning me this way and that.

"Well," she said at last, "as a pincushion I don't think much of it, but as a doll I think you've got something out of the ordinary. It isn't often you find a small one so perfectly made and with so much character. Why, I haven't got such a little gem in my whole collection."

I felt a pleasant sensation clear down to my buried wooden feet at her words. But I experienced even greater pleasure when I heard her friend say she would be only too glad to have her take me off her hands.

So Miss Pamela Wellington carried me home to join her famous collection of old dolls.

She made short work of removing the stuffings and silk that had been so carefully sewed about me. Her joy over finding my wooden legs and feet in perfect condition was second only to my own.

"It's just as I said," she told her maid. "As neat a pair of painted feet as you could ask for and the pegs working beautifully, and I declare if here isn't her name in cross-stitch."

She was as excited as a child and at once got out her piece-bag and began planning my new dress.

"How old do you reckon she is, Miss Pamela?" asked her maid, who took an almost equal interest in each addition to the collection.

"It's hard to say exactly," answered my new owner, tapping my wood with her forefinger and rubbing my face off very gently with a bit of chamois skin dampened in oil, "but she must be going on a hundred. I remember an aunt of mine had one of the same sort, though it didn't have half such a nicely carved face or so much expression."

"Yes, it certainly is the most human-looking of all your

dolls," agreed the maid, "real sweet, but up-and-coming, too."

I cannot tell the comfort I took in these words. Praise was very pleasant to me after my late junketings from pillar to post.

Miss Pamela dressed me herself in sprigged challis, copied after a dress she had worn as a child. Of course, she saw to it that my chemise was washed and pressed and darned where the linen was weakening a little. I became the favorite of all her collection. She kept me in a little old yellow rocker on her own writing desk and always showed me to visitors as her most prized doll. Her only regret was that she knew nothing of my history. She mourned this often and it made me wish more than ever that I had some way of telling her about myself. But even if she had not kept her ink bottle tightly corked and her paper stowed neatly away in cubby holes, there was no quill pen to help me write my story.

My only other regret of this period of my life is that I saw nothing of the other dolls; it would have been such an excellent opportunity to know my own kinsfolk better. There were hundreds of them all told on the shelves in the Wellington back parlor, and they were dressed in all manner of costumes from near and far.

As time went on, Miss Pamela grew more feeble, though she never admitted that she could not do so much as formerly. At last, one day, I heard her call the old servant to her and tell her that she had decided to go and spend the summer with an old friend in the country. She said that she would be motoring, so all the dolls must be left behind except me. I was small enough to go in her bag and she would miss having me on her desk. I was delighted at the idea of traveling once more, for I had not left her room for a number of years.

Unfortunately, I was packed in a satchel, which made it impossible to see where we were going. I knew, however, that sooner or later I should be settled in my new quarters. But before these were reached, I had an entirely new experience. Miss Pamela took me out of her bag for a few minutes while she hunted for a pair of gloves.

"Just hold this doll a minute, my dear," she said to her friend. "The car is going so fast I am afraid she will fly out."

Hardly had the words left her lips when this very thing happened to me. We were driving along a country road, but not behind the horses I had expected to see. No, instead, the carriage, which was neither high nor shaped as I remembered, seemed to be propelled by magic. The trees on either side of the road flew by with incredible swiftness, there was a steady purring noise under us, and the air went past faster even than the time the crow flew with me to the old pine. Just what happened I shall never know, but as the other old lady reached out to take me we went over a bump and I bounced from between their hands.

The next thing I knew was I was caught among some knotted tree roots, and I could hear the old ladies calling to a young man in a uniform, who began searching for me in every rut. He went up and down the road in vain, and Miss Pamela got out of the strange horseless carriage and looked, too. But though I could see them as plain as could be, they never thought of looking so far away for me. Besides, I was nearly out of sight between the mossy roots. It was bitter, indeed, to lie there and hear them drive away.

It was years, too, since I had been alone with the elements, not since the thunderstorm when Sally Loomis tossed me into the Mississippi, and a life of comfort and luxury unfits one for meeting such emergencies with fortitude.

My situation might have been far worse, however, for I had not fallen on my face but in a more or less upright position. The surrounding roots made a kind of deep chair for me and I could see quite a distance down the road and across a green and juniper-sprinkled pasture. The weather was warm. It must have been July, for the daisies and devil's paint brush made the fields and roadside very white and burnished. I could hear the sound of a brook rushing over stones not far off, and pine branches moved high overhead with a deep, familiar sound.

"If I could not stay with Miss Pamela always," I thought, "and if I must be left to wear away somewhere, at least this is as pleasant a spot as I could have chosen."

Night came on. The stars looked very pointed and far in the endless blue. The night air blew keen and strong from the other side of the pasture. Far, far off I caught a faint sound that seemed to me like surf beating somewhere. I wondered if this were so and if I should ever again look upon the ocean where I had once been as much at home as upon Miss Pamela's writing desk.

It was strange to see morning come over green and white fields and between needly boughs, after so many years of shutters and muslin curtains. My dress was soaked with the heavy dews, but the sun dried it again once it was high enough in the heavens to reach me. Birds swooped and sang. I found myself trying to remember their names from my old days on the Preble farm. Suddenly I realized that I had spent the latter part of my days in cities. Perhaps it was meant that I should return to the country again.

Little did I guess how truly I spoke—not, in fact, till a week or so later, when I was discovered and so came to know that I had, indeed, returned to my native State of Maine.

I shall pass lightly over the next years of my life, because, although I cannot in truth say that I knew actual suffering in them, still they were neither adventurous nor instructive. I moved from one place to another and knew no kind of security.

But to return to the pine roots near the road. I stayed there until some picnickers stopped to eat lunch under my tree. They were a noisy, unattractive lot of young men and women whose clothes shocked me by their tightness and lack of modesty. I would almost have preferred to stay unrescued than to fall into their hands. They joked and made all manner of foolish remarks about me and my appearance. One of the young men even set me on his knee and pretended to make love to me. This was not at all to my liking, though all the girls began to giggle. After they finished their lunch they took me back to the wagon with them. They had a real wagon with horses, the kind I was more used to. But many of the new-fangled affairs without them passed us. They referred to these as "automobiles."

Well, I need not have worried about belonging to this troupe, for when they returned the wagon to a stable where they had hired it, they forgot all about me. I was left sitting on the high back seat for a number of days. I rather enjoyed being in a stable again, and from the talk of the men who came and went I learned that I was in Maine again and not so very far from Portland.

I was discovered eventually when a party came to hire the carriage, and the stable man, not knowing what else to do with me, set me on the window ledge of his little office. It was rather hot there. The sun poured in and took most of the red that still remained in the pattern of my dress. Considerable dust gathered upon me, too, for it was a dry summer. The stable-owner was an oldish man, who had no opinion at all of automobiles. Nothing pleased him more than when one got stuck in the mud of a country road and he was called upon to drag it back with his ox team.

One day, his daughter came out to give his office its annual cleaning up. She couldn't understand how a little old wooden doll had come to be there among all the old harnesses, paint cans, whips, and fly-specked papers.

"Some child might like it, Pa," she said. "I believe I'll take it to Carrie's next time I go to Portland."

"Well, so do," he agreed, for he was eager to have her clear out of his room.

Carrie, I soon heard, was his married daughter, an enterprising woman who kept a little eating place on the Falmouth road. Every time I heard old names like that I was filled with pleasure. It seemed next best to meeting old friends. Sometimes I even entertained a wild hope that I might encounter Phoebe Preble again. But I knew that this was far from likely, for Miss Pamela had said I was "going on a hundred" and the flapping calendar in the stable office had told me that more years had passed than I had thought. There were still four figures in a row, but now there was a nine instead of an eight after the first one. Next, there had been another one and, last of all, a figure three. I was sorry that I had not known when the new century came in, but I supposed it must have happened while I was in the dead-letter office.

I was presently transferred to Carrie's restaurant on the Falmouth road, but she decided not to let her children play with me.

"I tell you, Bessie," she said to her sister, as they consumed large plates of cake and strawberries, "people are commencin' to give a lot for old things. I can't see the sense in it myself, but there was a man in here only last week lookin' at that old table I had in the kitchen. He scraped it with his knife and said 't was curly maple and there was some would pay as high as twenty dollars for it."

"Well, I think they're crazy," said her sister, "but it's all right if they're willin' to pay out good money. I don't feel, like Pa, that everything new must be wrong. Why don't you sell it, Carrie?"

"I mean to," she answered promptly. "I've been thinking it all over and I'm going to clear out the front parlor and cart in every old stick I have. You can send in anything you've got over to the farm and I'll have Jim make a sign saying 'Old Furniture for Sale.' This doll, now, you never can tell but some one might be foolish enough to buy it. I believe I'll see if I can get as much as a dollar for her."

Carrie was as good as her word and soon the front parlor looked, as her husband laughingly remarked, "like a regular junk heap." I sat upon a moth-eaten hassock and nobody took any special notice of me for what seemed to me like two or three years at least. Very little business went on in winter and the room was freezing. Summer, however, was a different matter. Finally, one day, a very diminutive old lady came in. She was so white-haired and pink-cheeked and she touched everything with such kindly, interested hands that I was reminded of Miss Pamela. I was therefore overjoyed when I saw her point to me and inquire my price.

"Oh, a couple of dollars, I guess," said Carrie, who was beginning to ask more now that people stopped oftener.

I felt quite weak in my pegs, fearing that the old lady would feel I was too expensive. She turned me about and moved my legs and arms to see if I was working perfectly.

"Well," she said to the woman who was with her, "I really came in to buy some china animals to go in the what-not, but there is something very appealing about this doll's expression."

"She may be an antique," said the other, "but I think she's ugly as sin."

So I was an antique! It was the first time I heard that word, which was to become such an everyday one to me later on. I was very grateful to the old lady for not agreeing with her friend. I hoped she would never regret the two dollars she handed over for me.

Even through the tissue paper I could tell that I was riding again in an automobile. I would have given much to see the country we drove through.

I fell to hoping that this old lady would have grandchildren who might perhaps like to play with me. This, however, was not to be. My next abode was in another parlor in a what-not full of bric-a-brac. My new owner lived alone with a maid and all her houseful of old furniture which people came from miles about to see. As I sat looking about me that first evening while the old lady read before the fireplace, something about the paneling and corner cupboards struck me as curiously famil-iar. There was a built-in preserve cupboard over the fireplace with a roughly cut letter "P" just above the latch. I stared at this incredulously, looked away, and then looked back again a number of times to make sure that my eyes had not gone back upon me. No, it was the same that I had seen so often during the first year of my life. I was in the Preble back parlor again after all these years. And as if the paneling and shape and letter "P" were not enough, there, sure enough, was the great trunk of the ancestral pine tree showing outside the window. I could even make out the very branch where I had hung. It seemed too amazing to believe. Yet here I was, and that night I sat listening to the wind moving in the pine boughs, making the same sound I remembered so well.

It was some time before I discovered how the old lady came to be living there. I knew she could not be Phoebe, but I wondered if she might turn out to be some relative. However, I heard her telling visitors one day that she knew nothing whatsoever about the house, though she had heard it once had belonged to a seafaring family by the name of Preble. She had been hunting for a place to house her old things, where she might also benefit by the bracing sea air in the summer. This had pleased her most of all she had seen, so she had had it slightly remodeled and moved in.

"Oh," thought I, as I heard her say this, "how much more I could tell her!"

My days with her were necessarily very quiet, for she saw only the visitors who came to view her collection and she never took me out on her hunts for more. Her particular passion was for small china animals of all sorts. Consequently, spotted dogs and cats, lambs, rabbits, setting hens, geese, gazelles, and porcelain pigs were all about me in the what-not. I sometimes used to feel that I had entered a menagerie and I

I sometimes used to feel that I had entered a menagerie.

was in despair over each new addition. I suppose it must have been my contacts with live animals in the past that made me so critical of these chilly, china counterparts. I could not but remember the wise eyes and quick hands of the Island monkeys and the warm, moist tongues of the obliging mice in the hayloft.

This I used to think of especially in winter when the house was shut up tight and the old lady had left for her stay in the city. The Preble parlor had no cheerful fire in it then, and through chinks in the shutters I could see snow and ice outside. Sometimes, when the wind was in the right direction, I could hear the church bell ringing. I was sure it must be the one on Meeting House Hill and I wondered if the wooden footstool and the old illustrated Bible were still under the pew where I had once lain. So for a number of winters I entertained myself with memories of the past as I waited for spring and the old lady to return.

It was good to have the doors and windows flung open after the winter, and the lilacs were almost always sure to be out in deep purple spikes of bloom on either side of the front door. From my place I could see out past the pine toward the orchard where the apple trees were only a trifle more gnarled and crooked and their blossoms pinker than I remembered. Yes, shrubs and day lilies, moss roses, and honeysuckle grew as thick in the dooryard as they had grown when Phoebe Preble went out to pick them with me in her apron pocket. I even heard crows making the same noisy racket in the upper branches of the old pine and I fell to wondering if they were the great-great-something-or-others of those baby crows whose nest I had so unwillingly shared.

# CHAPTER XVII
## In Which I Am Sold at Auction

But one year spring came just as usual and the old lady did not. I could not understand it, and it seemed a pity she should not see how fine the lilacs were. Indeed, all summer passed and there was not a sign of her. If it had not been for the chinks in the shutters I should not have known when the roses were at their height nor seen the goldenrod beginning.

Then at last in September the doors were unlocked and a number of men came in. I had never seen any of them before, but they made themselves very much at home. They tramped about the different rooms, turning everything upside down and handling furniture and ornaments in a way I am sure the old lady would have disliked. They had a great many small tags with numbers on them, which they fastened to every chair, table, and picture, even to the china animals and me. Mine was hung round my neck, and before they put it on I made out that the number was seventy-seven.

"Well, Frank," I heard one of them say to the fattest of the group, "we've numbered all the stuff upstairs and it ought to bring good priccs."

"Ought to if we get a good day," the fat man said, squinting from the doorway at the sun just setting behind the spruce trees across the road, "and it looks promising. Summer visitors'll come from miles round, or I miss my guess."

"Yes, sir," said another, as they gathered up their papers and pencils, "this is going to be one of the liveliest auctions ever held in these parts. Antiques, that's what they've all gone crazy over nowadays."

Their words filled me with vague misgivings and whenever I forgot them for a few minutes I was sure to feel the square of numbered cardboard hanging round my own neck. The only cause I had for cheerfulness was that I had been removed from the collection of china animals. Those had been divided into lots according to their kind and they were evidently not considered important enough to have each a separate number.

The men arrived bright and early next morning. It was as fine a day in early fall as I have ever seen. There was more tramping about and the pieces of furniture from the second-floor rooms were all carried down and set out on the front lawn. I had a better place of vantage now from a chest in the front hall, so I could see motor cars beginning to arrive from every direction. Before ten o'clock the road was blocked with them and the yard and house overflowed with chattering groups of people. I could not but be rather startled by their appearance, especially that of the women and children. They seemed to have on almost no clothes to speak of. I could not help feeling it was just as well that Mrs. Preble could not see them making so free of all the corners of her house. She would have lifted her hands in horror at the sight of children with bare legs and arms and brief dresses, and ladies with hair and skirts almost as short.

I was soon being handled by these curious hordes, who tipped me upside down, moved my arms and legs, and pried at my petticoats and pantalettes in a very rude way.

"Antique, antique, antique," I heard the word on every side, till I began to think the man had been right yesterday about people having gone crazy on this subject.

There were several people in the crowd who treated me after a better fashion. One of these was a pretty little girl in a yellow dress and big straw hat. She seemed less noisy and fidgety than the others, more like the little girls I had known in the past. She could not have been more than six, for the lady with her had to lift me down for her to get a good look at me.

"I want her, Auntie," begged the little girl, "and I have the dollar that Daddy gave me right here in my purse. Don't you think that would be enough? She is so little and tanned."

The lady laughed.

"It's because her paint is off, Molly," she said, "and her number is seventy-seven, so it will be quite a while before they get to her."

"I want her," insisted the child, "and she *is* tanned."

Her words did much to sustain me through this trying ordeal, as did the sprig of mignonette which she put in my lap.

Besides, there was the Old Gentleman in the gray suit, with the pointed white beard and the single round glass dangling from a ribbon. This he would screw into his eye when he studied anything carefully. He looked at me through it for a long time, turning me about between a very long, kindly thumb and forefinger. Nothing escaped him, not even the cross-stitch letters on my innermost garment, but somehow one did not mind his curiosity. Indeed, I was greatly flattered by the length of time he spent over me and the number of times he screwed the glass into his eye as he looked me over.

"That," he said finally, setting me back carefully on the

chest and turning to a gentleman standing beside him, "is a very rare bit of early Americana."

He moved off to another room, but not before the fat man of the day before had overheard his words. I saw him scribble something down on a long list he carried and also whisper a word to one of his companions. He jerked his thumb in my direction, so I was sure it had something to do with me. But still I could not make out what was going to happen, for I had never heard of an auction before.

It was not long, however, before I found out.

The people flocked out into the front yard once more, sitting on camp chairs, old boxes, and anything else they could find. The fat man took his place on the doorstep behind what had been the kitchen table and his friends came forward with a trayful of the china dogs. These were set down before him and it was something of a shock to see him lift a big hammer in one hand. Just for a moment I thought he meant to smash them then and there, and I felt frightened for myself, but not, I must confess, especially sorry at the thought of seeing the china animals broken.

I soon learned my mistake when the auctioneer called for bids and the people in front began calling out what they were willing to give. Things were rather slow at first; the china dogs did not turn out to be so popular as the fat man had expected. The lot was finally knocked down for five dollars and the auctioneer shook his head and said it was a crime, that's what it was. Sometimes a good many people wanted the same thing and that made it very exciting. They bid against each other and the fat man encouraged them by pounding with his hammer and raising the price every few minutes.

One other thing came as a surprise to me—that certain objects which I had more or less taken for granted were in great demand. A copper teakettle that I had never thought of as belonging anywhere but on a kitchen stove brought a large sum, and some old fire tongs and the iron crane and chains brought even more. I certainly thought it was fortunate the Prebles were not about to witness such goings-on in their front yard.

Well, my turn came at last, and I do not believe anyone will blame me much for having strange misgivings and tremors in my pegs. After my number was called, I was carried out to the table and set on a wooden box in front of the Auctioneer. I kept one hand on the sprig of mignonette and with the other tried to anchor down my skirts. Even though I was to be auctioned off, I meant to keep my dignity. It was about noon now, a little breeze stirred the branches of the old pine above us, and across the road the sun was bright on asters and goldenrod. It was the first time I had been outdoors since my return to my birthplace and I felt suddenly moved by the sight of so many familiar sights. Yet the strange faces were staring at me, laughter and whispered words went from mouth to mouth, as the fat man raised his hammer.

"Ladies and gentlemen," he began, "I have before me item seventy-seven—"

He paused to consult his paper, and a ripple of amused interest swept through the crowd.

"Hitty!" I suddenly heard the little girl cry. "Her name's Hitty. It says so on her underclothes."

Everyone laughed at that, even the Auctioneer.

"Well," he went on, looking up from his paper, "that makes

her just a little more valuable, I guess. I am sure you have all observed her and seen that she is in perfect condition, no legs or arms missing—fully clothed, and I might be so bold to add that from her expression she appears to be in her right mind." Another burst of laughter from the crowd, but the little girl was standing on a soap box with a very determined expression and her dollar in her hand. "What some of you may not know is that she is a rare bit of Americana." He read the words off quickly from his paper and I thought to myself that he would not have known it either except for the Old Gentleman in the gray clothes. "Well, ladies and gentlemen, how much am I offered for the doll Hitty, over a hundred years old, a rare antique that anyone might be proud to have in the family?"

"Here," cried the little girl, without waiting for him to finish, "here's my dollar."

"One dollar," began the fat man in his droning voice that he always used as soon as the bidding started, "one dollar is the bid for this rare doll. Who'll raise the bid to two dollars?"

"Two—two—two-fifty," I heard the bids coming in from different directions.

Some one pressed forward and shut the little girl's face out of sight. I was almost glad, for I knew she must be disappointed. In a way, I was, too; I should like to have belonged to her and yet I could not but begin to take pride in the way the bids were coming in.

"Ten dollars," some one in the second row was offering.

"Ten dollars," repeated the fat man witheringly, "only ten dollars. Why, ladies and gentlemen, don't you know a rare piece of Americana when you meet it?"

"Fifteen dollars," I heard from the last row.

I did not like the sound of the loud voice, but I liked still less the owner of it. She was a very large lady in a tight pink dress and bright green hat. This she wore pulled down over a mass of hair that stuck out in a bush about her far too rosy face, much as the Savage Chief's had done on the Island. Indeed, she reminded me of him strongly. The word "rare" seemed to affect her strangely. I almost wished the Auctioneer had not used it to describe me.

But the Old Gentleman came to my rescue. I could see him standing a little at one side, near the trunk of the old pine. His hat was off and the upper branches made shadow patternings on his white hair and beard. I thought I detected an amused, yet determined, expression about his lips.

"Sixteen dollars," he bid deliberately and put his cigar back between them.

"Twenty dollars!" cried the lady promptly.

"Twenty-one," added her rival, hardly raising his voice at all.

And so it went. All other bidders had dropped out by this time and everyone listened to see which of them would hold out the longer.

"Twenty-five dollars, ladies and gentlemen," I heard the droning tones of the fat man going on above me, "the lady in the back row offers me twenty-five dollars for the doll."

I looked over in her direction again and all my fears were doubled. She looked more like the Savage Chief than ever, now that she was getting so heated and making such faces. It seemed to me that to fall into her hands would be more than I could bear.

"Twenty-six fifty," came the reassuring voice of the Old Gentleman.

"Thirty!" cried the other shrilly, and then she added in a voice that could be heard plainly, "I mean to have it if I go to fifty."

After that it settled down into a regular contest, with the woman sending my price soaring and the other quietly adding just a dollar more each time. Even the Auctioneer showed signs of excitement and all the rest watched and listened breathlessly. I am sure no slave on the block was ever more surprised at her own value than I. When I heard it going past forty, I could scarcely credit my own hearing. The Old Peddler little dreamed when he was fashioning me so long ago that I should ever bring such a sum, and he knew that I was made of mountain-ash wood. Somehow I got so upset in my mind sitting there with all this going on that I began to confuse the Old Gentleman under the pine with the Peddler. There was something strangely alike about them. But I roused myself in time to see the woman brandishing a bead bag and calling out even more shrilly than before:

"I make it fifty dollars!"

A shocked gasp went round before the Auctioneer took up her bid.

"Fifty dollars," he began solemnly, "I am offered fifty dollars. Does any lady or gentleman wish to add anything to this bid?"

There was no sound from my friend under the pine. The smoke curled up from his cigar and his round glass was in his eye. Not a flicker did he make.

"Fifty dollars," the fat man was sing-songing above me. "Fifty dollars once—fifty dollars twice—"

He raised his hammer high in the air and every eye was fixed on it.

But as I looked out over the crowd I saw the woman in her tight pink dress had turned to speak to the man beside her. She felt so sure of me that she did not bother to see me knocked down, so taking the arm of the man, she moved off toward a blue and glistening motor car.

"For the third time—fifty dol—" began the Auctioneer.

"Fifty-one dollars," I heard a voice say from the pine tree, and I knew that I was saved.

"Fifty-one dollars," the fat man was repeating, but the woman was safely out of earshot now.

"Fifty-one dollars once—fifty-one dollars twice—fifty-one dollars three times. "

This time the hammer came down so vigorously that I toppled off the box and backward on the table. But I was too relieved to feel humiliated, even when everyone burst out laughing. The Old Gentleman came forward, and a cheer actually went up as he straightened my clothes. Never since my days on the Island have I felt more grateful for an escape.

I was rather overcome by the varied emotions of the morning and glad that my new owner arranged to take me away with him before the finish of the auction. There was to be an interval for lunch and I feared the woman would try to get me into her clutches again, so I was happy to see him pay one of the men, gather up his hat and a small bag, and leave.

He stopped just long enough to wrap me in his figured-silk handkerchief and put me in the breast pocket of his coat. It was considerate of him to leave my head out. It seemed as if he must have guessed how much a walk down the old road would mean to me. He walked briskly and refused a number of rides that motorists offered us.

It was just such a blue September day as the one when I had driven with the Prebles to Portland to take the Boston stage. There was the same light on every leaf and berry and grass blade, and the wooded islands looked dark and twinkling in distant blue water. Except for an added house or two, strange ships in the harbor, and the cars flashing by us, I could not see that things had changed much since Phoebe Preble's day. Yet they had said that was a hundred years ago. All my adventures were very clear to me then. They seemed to be connected with the fall colors on every side—the gold and purple of roadside flowers and the scarlets and yellows and tawny browns of the trees we passed. I even saw some mountain-ash berries showing orange in the sun.

After a while, the Old Gentleman boarded a train and we rode through more autumn colors and scenes. We had been traveling a long while before he opened his bag to put me in.

"Well, young lady," he said a little sternly, though I could see that he did not really mean it, because his lips were smiling, "you cost me a pretty penny today. Do you honestly think you're worth the hooked rug, the china tea set, and the windsor chair I went there to buy?"

Just as he was closing the bag, our train must have crossed the State line into New Hampshire, for he pointed this out to me and added, "You're beginning your travels now, Hitty. I don't suppose you were ever out of the State of Maine before."

"And that," I thought to myself, as he shut me in, "only goes to show that even the wisest people don't know everything."

# Last Remarks

And so we return to New York and the Antique Shop on Eighth Street again, and I will bring my Memoirs to a close. High time I did, too, for patience and paper are giving out.

How did I get here from the Old Gentleman's bag and the train from Maine? Well, that is easily explained. He had been told by Miss Hunter to buy some old things for her shop. I think he was a little wadgetty when it came to showing her that I was all he had for the money. But she did not seem to mind and together they exclaimed over my size, features, and expression.

"A real museum piece," she declared with enthusiasm.

"I can't seem to make out her wood," the Old Gentleman said, "it's not maple or hickory or pine."

"Well, whatever it is, she's worn well," Miss Hunter pronounced, when she had been over every inch of me. "Over a hundred years old and working perfectly."

"More than we'll be able to say for ourselves," he added with a smile as he picked up his bag to leave.

But that was not the last I saw of him. In fact, he was in only yesterday to bring me a little pine bench. Hardly ever does he return from one of his collecting trips without some present for me—a tiny braided rug, a shell, and a miniature four-post bedstead. Miss Hunter says he spoils me disgracefully. Sometimes she hides me when she sees him coming and says she has sold me since the last time he was in. But they are far from anxious to part with me. Customers say my price is scandalous, even for an antique.

In a small way I have become quite well known in the neighborhood. Miss Hunter has pinned a paper with my name on the front of my dress. This was a great relief to me, as I grew tired of being explored by so many strange fingers. As I sit on my shelf among my personal effects, I often hear comments passed upon me through the glass. Many passersby even call

I feel that many more adventures are awaiting me.

me by name. I understand that two artists in particular are often heard to remark when they are out walking: "Let's go home by the Antique Shop and say how-do-you-do to Hitty." So I sit and look out at these more discerning ones with my pleasant expression, which has perhaps grown slightly faint with the years but has never failed me in any emergency.

My days here are not without proper enlivenment. Each new customer who enters the shop fills me with interest and suspense, for who knows but this may be the one fated to carry me away to further adventures? I feel that many more are awaiting me. Only the other morning I heard a curious purring noise high in the air and saw people stop to look up. In my efforts to do likewise I tumbled off the bench and onto my back on the shelf. This position, however, gave me an excellent view of the sky above the buildings, and there I saw what appeared to be a gigantic dragon-fly with silvery wings swooping and sporting in the blue.

"Oh, see the airplane!" cried a little child out on the sidewalk, "I mean to fly in one some day."

I watched it out of sight with a sense of wonder and anticipation. Perhaps, like the child on the sidewalk I, too, shall take to the air. Why not, since the world is always arranging new experiences for us, and I have never felt more hale and hearty in my life? After all, what is a mere hundred years to well-seasoned mountain-ash wood?

# Also by Rachel Field

A NEWBERY HONOR BOOK

Left orphaned and alone in a strange country, thirteen-year-old Marguerite Ledoux has no choice but to become a servant girl for a family she has never met. Living in an isolated part of northern Maine, Maggie struggles through the harsh, hungry winter of 1743, the constant threat of Indian attack, and worst of all, the loneliness she suffers knowing that her own family is lost forever. Will the Sargent's house ever feel like home?

"*Calico Bush* is a story of the first rank"—*New York Times*

# Hitty's adventures continue!

Look for a new, full-color adaptation of Hitty's life story on the seventieth anniversary of the original's publication! The intrepid wooden doll, lovingly portrayed by Rosemary Wells and Susan Jeffers, is exposed to even more important events in American history.

**RACHEL FIELD'S HITTY with New Adventures**
by Rosemary Wells, illustrated by Susan Jeffers
Simon & Schuster Books for Young Readers

Simon & Schuster Children's Publishing Division
where imaginations meet
www.SimonSaysKids.com

# HAVE YOU READ ALL OF THE ALICE BOOKS?

## PHYLLIS REYNOLDS NAYLOR

STARTING WITH ALICE
Atheneum Books for
  Young Readers
  0-689-84395-X
Aladdin Paperbacks
  0-689-84396-8

ALICE IN BLUNDERLAND
Atheneum Books for
  Young Readers
  0-689-84397-6

LOVINGLY ALICE
Atheneum Books for
  Young Readers
  0-689-84399-2

THE AGONY OF ALICE
Atheneum Books for
  Young Readers
  0-689-31143-5
Aladdin Paperbacks
  0-689-81672-3

ALICE IN RAPTURE,
  SORT-OF
Atheneum Books for
  Young Readers
  0-689-31466-3
Aladdin Paperbacks
  0-689-81687-1

RELUCTANTLY ALICE
Atheneum Books for
  Young Readers
  0-689-31681-X
Aladdin Paperbacks
  0-689-81688-X

ALL BUT ALICE
Atheneum Books for
Young Readers
  0-689-31773-5
Aladdin Paperbacks
  0-689-85044-1

ALICE IN APRIL
Atheneum Books for
  Young Readers
  0-689-31805-7
Aladdin Paperbacks
  0-689-81686-3

ALICE IN-BETWEEN
Atheneum Books for
  Young Readers
  0-689-31890-0
Aladdin Paperbacks
  0-689-81685-5

ALICE THE BRAVE
Atheneum Books for
  Young Readers
  0-689-80095-9
Aladdin Paperbacks
  0-689-80598-5

ALICE IN LACE
Atheneum Books for
  Young Readers
  0-689-80358-3
Aladdin Paperbacks
  0-689-80597-7

OUTRAGEOUSLY ALICE
Atheneum Books for
  Young Readers
  0-689-80354-0
Aladdin Paperbacks
  0-689-80596-9

ACHINGLY ALICE
Atheneum Books for
  Young Readers
  0-689-80533-9
Aladdin Paperbacks
  0-689-80595-0
Simon Pulse
  0-689-86396-9

ALICE ON THE OUTSIDE
Atheneum Books for
  Young Readers
  0-689-80359-1
Simon Pulse
  0-689-80594 2

GROOMING OF ALICE
Atheneum Books for
  Young Readers
  0-689-82633-8
Simon Pulse
  0-689-84618-5

ALICE ALONE
Atheneum Books for
  Young Readers
  0-689-82634-6
Simon Pulse
  0-689-85189-8

SIMPLY ALICE
Atheneum Books for
  Young Readers
  0-689-84751-3
Simon Pulse
  0-689-85965-1

PATIENTLY ALICE
Atheneum Books for
  Young Readers
  0-689-82636-2
Simon Pulse
  0-689-87073-6

INCLUDING ALICE
Atheneum Books for
  Young Readers
  0-689-82637-0

The Newbery Medal is awarded each year to the most distinguished contribution to literature for children published in the U.S. How many of these Newbery winners, available from Aladdin and Simon Pulse, have you read?

## NEWBERY MEDAL WINNERS

❏ *King of the Wind*
by Marguerite Henry
0-689-71486-6

❏ *M.C. Higgins, the Great*
by Virginia Hamilton
0-02-043490-1

❏ *Caddie Woodlawn*
by Carol Ryrie Brink
0-689-81521-2

❏ *Call It Courage*
by Armstrong Sperry
0-02-045270-5

❏ *The Cat Who Went
to Heaven*
by Elizabeth Coatsworth
0-698-71433-5

❏ *From the Mixed-up
Files of Mrs. Basil E.
Frankweiler*
by E. L. Konigsburg
0-689-71181-6

❏ *A Gathering of Days*
by Joan W. Blos
0-689-71419-X

❏ *The Grey King*
by Susan Cooper
0-689-71089-5

❏ *Hitty: Her First
Hundred Years*
by Rachel Field
0-689-82284-7

❏ *Mrs. Frisby and the
Rats of NIMH*
by Robert C. O'Brien
0-689-71068-2

❏ *Shadow of a Bull*
by Maia Wojciechowska
0-689-71567-6

❏ *Smoky the Cow
Horse*
by Eric P. Kelly
0-689-71682-6

❏ *The View from
Saturday*
by E. L. Konigsburg
0-689-81721-5

❏ *Dicey's Song*
by Cynthia Voigt
0-689-81721-5

Paperbacks Books • Simon & Schuster Children's Publishing
www.SimonSaysKids.com

The Newbery Medal is awarded each year to the most distinguished contribution to literature for children published in the U.S. How many of these honor books, available from Aladdin Paperbacks, have you read?

## NEWBERY HONOR BOOKS

❏ *The Bears on Hemlock Mountain*
by Alice Dalgliesh
0-689-71604-4

❏ *Misty of Chincoteague*
by Marguerite Henry
0-689-71492-0

❏ *Calico Bush*
by Rachel Field
0-689-82285-5

❏ *The Courage of Sarah Noble*
by Alice Dalgliesh
0-689-71540-4

❏ *The Dark Is Rising*
by Susan Cooper
0-689-71087-9

❏ *Dogsong*
by Gary Paulsen
0-689-80409-1

❏ *The Golden Fleece*
by Padraic Colum
0-02-042260-1

❏ *The Moorchild*
by Eloise McGraw
0-689-82033-X

❏ *Hatchet*
by Gary Paulsen
0-689-80882-8

❏ *The Jazz Man*
by Mary Hays Weik
0-689-71767-9

❏ *Justin Morgan Had a Horse*
by Marguerite Henry
0-689-71534-X

❏ *The Planet of Junior Brown*
by Virginia Hamilton
0-689-71721-0

❏ *A String in the Harp*
by Nancy Bond
0-689-80445-8

❏ *Sugaring Time*
by Kathryn Lasky
0-689-71081-X

❏ *Volcano*
by Patricia Lauber
0-689-71679-6

❏ *Yolonda's Genius*
by Carol Fenner
0-689-81327-9

Aladdin Paperbacks • Simon & Schuster Children's Publishing
www.SimonSaysKids.com

# The past comes ALIVE

## in stirring historical fiction from
## ALADDIN PAPERBACKS

☐ **The Best Bad Thing**
Yoshiko Uchida
0-689-71745-8

☐ **Fever 1793**
Laurie Halse Anderson
0-689-83858-1

☐ **The Journey Home**
Yoshiko Uchida
0-689-71641-9

☐ **Shades of Gray**
Carolyn Reeder
0-689-82696-6

☐ **Brothers of the Heart**
Joan W. Blos
0-689-71724-5

☐ **Forty Acres and Maybe a Mule**
Harriette Gillem Robinet
0-689-83317-2

☐ **The Journey to America Saga**
Sonia Levitin
*Annie's Promise*
0-689-80440-7
*Journey to America*
0-689-71130-1
*Silver Days*
0-689-71570-6

☐ **Steal Away Home**
Lois Ruby
0-689-82435-1

☐ **Caddie Woodlawn**
Carol Ryrie Brink
0-689-71370-3

☐ **A Gathering of Days**
Joan W. Blos
0-689-71419-X

☐ **Under the Shadow of Wings**
Sara Harrell Banks
0-689-82436-X

☐ **The Eternal Spring of Mr. Ito**
Sheila Garrigue
0-689-71809-8

☐ **A Jar of Dreams**
Yoshiko Uchida
0-689-71672-9

☐ **The Second Mrs. Giaconda**
E. L. Konigsburg
0-689-82121-2

# ALADDIN CLASSICS

## ALL THE BEST BOOKS FOR CHILDREN
## AND THEIR FAMILIES TO READ!

**THE SECRET GARDEN**
by Frances Hodgson Burnett
Foreword by E. L. Konigsburg
0-689-83141-2

**TREASURE ISLAND**
by Robert Louis Stevenson
Foreword by Avi
0-689-83212-5

**ALICE'S ADVENTURES IN
WONDERLAND**
by Lewis Carroll
Foreword by Nancy Willard
0-689-83375-X

**LITTLE WOMEN**
by Louisa May Alcott
Foreword by Joan W. Blos
0-689-83531-0

**THE HOUND OF THE BASKERVILLES**
by Sir Arthur Conan Doyle
Foreword by Bruce Brooks
0-689-83571-X

**THE WIND IN THE WILLOWS**
by Kenneth Grahame
Foreword by Susan Cooper
0-689-83140-4

**THE WIZARD OF OZ**
by L. Frank Baum
Foreword by Eloise McGraw
0-689-83142-0

**THE ADVENTURES OF
HUCKLEBERRY FINN**
by Mark Twain
Foreword by Gary Paulsen
0-689-83139-0

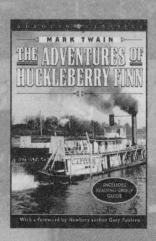

**ALADDIN PAPERBACKS**
SIMON & SCHUSTER CHILDREN'S PUBLISHING • www.SimonSaysKids.com

# ALADDIN CLASSICS

*THE CALL OF THE WILD*
by Jack London
Foreword by Gary Paulsen
0-689-85674-1

*HEIDI*
by Johanna Spyri
Foreword by Eloise McGraw
0-689-83962-6

*THE RAVEN AND OTHER
WRITINGS*
by Edgar Allan Poe
Foreword by Avi
0-689-86352-7

*A CHRISTMAS CAROL*
by Charles Dickens
Foreword by Nancy Farmer
0-689-87180-5

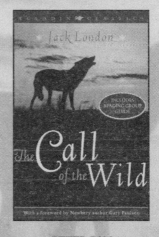

*PETER PAN*
by J.M. Barrie
Foreword by Susan Cooper
0-689-86691-7

*ANNE OF GREEN GABLES*
by L. M. Montgomery
Foreword by Katherine Paterson
0-689-84622-3

*A LITTLE PRINCESS*
by Frances Hodgson Burnett
Foreword by Nancy Bond
0-689-84407-7

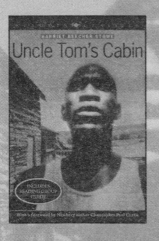

*UNCLE TOM'S CABIN*
by Harriet Beecher Stowe
Foreword by
Christopher Paul Curtis
0-689-85126-X